I've travelled the world twice over,
Met the famous: saints and sinners,
Poets and artists, kings and queens,
Old stars and hopeful beginners,
I've been where no-one's been before,
Learned secrets from writers and cooks
All with one library ticket
To the wonderful world of books.

© JANICE JAMES.

THE LEATHER DUKE

Circumstances beyond their control (and for once, beyond their ability to twist, sidestep, or disregard) force Johnny Fletcher and Sam Cragg to take jobs. They become the employees of 'The Leather Duke', Chicago's biggest operator in the leather business. But before they've been there half a day, Sam finds a corpse. Then the uproar begins. Whether they're fighting in poolrooms, mixing it up at dances, or merely adding to their well-developed art of deadbeating, these two lads are at it every minute.

FRANK GRUBER

◆

THE LEATHER DUKE

Complete and Unabridged

ULVERSCROFT
Leicester

First published in the
United States of America

First Large Print Edition
published 1996

British Library CIP Data

Gruber, Frank
    The leather duke.—Large print ed.—
Ulverscroft large print series: mystery
I. Title
823.912 [F]

ISBN 0–7089–3485–4

Published by
F. A. Thorpe (Publishing) Ltd.
Anstey, Leicestershire
Set by Words & Graphics Ltd.
Anstey, Leicestershire
Printed and bound in Great Britain by
T. J. Press (Padstow) Ltd., Padstow, Cornwall

This book is printed on acid-free paper

1

MORT MURRAY was the cause of it all. Mort Murray, publisher of *Every Man A Samson*, the book that had earned a livelihood for Johnny Fletcher and Sam Cragg for so many years. Mort Murray, that Rock of Gibraltar, that lighthouse on the rocky shore, that friend-in-need-is-a-friend-indeed.

Mort Murray had let them down. In their hour of need, he had failed Johnny Fletcher and Sam Cragg. Yes, he had failed to pay his rent and the sheriff had put a padlock on his door. So he had been unable to send the books that Johnny had ordered by Western Union, collect.

And now Johnny and Sam were walking the streets of Chicago homeless and hungry. They had caught fitful snatches of sleep in the Northwestern and Union Depots, but you can't really get a good night's repose in those places. The benches are hard and there are always policemen and station attendants to annoy you.

Things were bad.

Silently, Johnny and Sam turned north on Larrabee Street and silently they walked past the dingy factory buildings of the near North Side. People were working in those buildings, lifting barrels, wrestling crates and cartons, and operating whirring machines. It rained and snowed; sometimes the wind howled and sometimes the sun shone brightly. But those people in the buildings were oblivious to it all. They came to work at eight o'clock in the morning, they toiled all day and at five o'clock they went home. They went to work in these factories as boys and girls, they fell in love and were married. They raised children and the children in their turn went to work in the same factories. There was no end to it. Oh, yes, they changed jobs sometimes, these workers. They quit one factory and went into another. The work was the same, more or less, the pay was the same, a little more or less, and the hours never changed.

"Sam," Johnny Fletcher said, as they

walked along, "we've got to get a job."

"Sure," agreed Sam, then ten seconds later came to a complete halt. "*What did you say, Johnny?*"

"I said we've got to get a job. We're up against it. I've thought and I've thought and I can't see any way out of it. We've got to get a stake, and the only way is to get a job."

"But, Johnny!" cried Sam. "You've never done any work, you've never held a job in your whole life . . . "

Johnny exhaled heavily. "Oh, yes, I have. In my youth, I had two jobs — not one, two. I worked in a grocery store once, delivering orders and another time — for five weeks — I worked in a bowling alley, setting up pins. What about you — have *you* ever worked?"

"Me? Oh, sure, before I started wrestling I had a job for a year, driving a truck."

"What kind of a truck?"

"A sand and gravel truck. Sometimes I hauled a load of cement. That was easy, unloading those little hundred-pound sacks of cement."

"Then this job ought to be a cinch."

3

"Which job?"

Johnny pointed at a squat, five-story building across the street. "Towner Leather Company," he read. "There's a sign next to the door, Man Wanted."

A shudder ran through Sam's body. "No, Johnny, no," he whispered hoarsely. "Not a leather factory."

"What's wrong with leather? It's one of the most useful articles in the world. They make shoes with it. And the harness the farmers use on their horses is made of leather. Why, if it wasn't for leather, the farmers couldn't drive their horses and if they couldn't drive horses, they couldn't plow ground to raise potatoes and corn and wheat. No, Sam, we couldn't live without leather."

"Sure, Johnny, I admit it. Leather's important. I've got nothing against leather. It's just . . . well, work . . . ! We've been together a long time, Johnny. Twelve years. In all that time we ain't never had to work before. You always figured out something."

"I know, but I've been thinking lately — maybe I've been wrong. Maybe it isn't right not to work. Look at all these

4

people in these buildings; they're not walking the streets. They've got homes, they get three square meals a day. They save their money and when they get old they can quit working . . . "

"You mean they work like hell so they can quit working?"

"That's right."

"That shows how silly it is, Johnny. Why should we work all our lives, just so we can quit working? We're not working now."

"Your argument's sound, Sam, but we haven't had breakfast and we didn't have dinner yesterday. Not to mention lunch. So we're going in here and get a job."

"Yeah, but it says Man Wanted, Johnny, *man*, not *men*. That means one, doesn't it? Uh, which of us is going to take that job?"

"We could toss for it, if we had a coin, but since we haven't, why not leave it to the gods? Or the foreman or whatever they call the fellow who hires men. We'll both go in and ask for the job and whoever he picks, why that's it."

"But don't you think he'd pick the first one to go in?"

5

"We'll go in together. We'll play it fair, right down the line. If I get the job I'll meet you out here at five o'clock with the money and if you get it, I'll be waiting for you. That's fair, isn't it?"

"I suppose so," conceded Sam, "but I've got an awful hunch that I'm going to be the sucker."

He drew a deep breath, let it out slowly, then followed Johnny into the building of the Towner Leather Company.

Inside, a short flight of stairs led to a glass-paneled door. Johnny pushed open this second door and they found themselves in an office where thirty or forty office workers toiled at various desks.

Immediately in front of them a young woman sat at a desk, which contained a small switchboard. She had taffy-colored hair, very nice features and plenty of what a girl ought to have. She looked inquiringly at Johnny and he brightened.

"Well, well," he said, "this is a little better than I expected."

"And what did you expect?" the girl asked coolly. "A two-headed octopus?"

"*Touché*," exclaimed Johnny, "or as

6

we say in Brooklyn, touch. I'm making a survey of what lonely men in Chicago do. Lonely men, who are strangers in town. Suppose this was Saturday night; where would such a man go for a little entertainment and, shall we say, fun?"

"Depends on the lonely man's financial condition," the girl said.

"Suppose we say the man has a — a couple of bucks?"

"Two dollars, eh? Then I guess he'd go to the Clybourn Dance Hall, or the Bucket of Blood as we call it on Clybourn Avenue."

"Bucket of Blood, eh? Charming name. Mmm, well, suppose said lonely man had a larger stake, say about twenty bucks, where would they go then?"

"Oh, in that case he could go to the College Inn, or the Edgewater Beach Hotel, or even the Chez Hogan, on East Rush Street. Provided, of course, that he had a girl."

"Ah yes, the girl. That's important. But how could said lonely man who was a stranger in town find said girl to accompany him to said night spots?"

"Why, I guess he could stand on a

street corner and whistle at the girls who passed. He'd probably get a few slaps in the face, he'd likely wind up in jail, but he might, he might just possibly get a girl and it would serve him right if he did. Now, mister, are there any other questions you want to ask?"

"Yes, what do they call you around here?"

"They call me, 'hey you,' on account of my name is Nancy Miller. Now, fun's fun, but I've got work to do. Now, what are you selling and who is it you'd like to have say no?"

"Get ready for a surprise, Nancy. We're selling — us." Johnny beamed at the girl, who looked at him sharply. "There's a little old sign outside the door. It says 'Man Wanted.'"

"Oh, Mister!" cried Nancy Miller. "So you're looking for a job!"

"*He* is," chimed in Sam Cragg. "*I'm* not."

Johnny ignored Sam. "Sure, Nancy, how else am I going to get that twenty dollars by Saturday?"

"You could get a loan on your Cadillac."

"If I had a Cadillac. Ha ha! No foolin', Taffy, we need a job badly. How's about giving us the lowdown on this one?"

"Oh, I don't mind. I don't mind at all. This is a working job. You actually do things with your hands. The pay is thirty-two dollars — "

"Thirty-two bucks!" cried Johnny.

" — For a forty-hour week. But as you actually work forty-four hours you get thirty-six-fifty a week . . . "

"That isn't very much."

"No," exclaimed Sam. "It ain't. In fact, we couldn't work that cheap, so thanks just the same."

Johnny regarded him coldly. "How much are we making a week now?" He turned back to Nancy Miller. "A man's got to start somewhere. A big place like this I suppose there's a chance for advancement . . . "

"Oh, certainly. You stick to the job and work hard you can be making thirty-eight, forty dollars a week, in no time at all. Say, about six years."

Sam groaned, but Johnny nodded gloomily. "We'll take the job."

"What do you mean, we? There's only

one job vacant. Which of you wants it? And *I* don't do the hiring. It's Mr. Johnson who has the opening . . . Do you want to see him?"

"We who are about to die, salute you!" Johnny said. "In short, yes, we'll see your Mr. Johnson and" — looking at Sam — "may the best man win."

The girl shook her head and made a connection on the switchboard. After a moment she said into the phone: "Mr. Johnson, there are a couple of men here asking about that job . . . Mmm, yes, all right . . . Thank you, I'll tell them." She broke the connection. "He'll be right down."

"He asked if we looked okay, didn't he?" asked Johnny.

"There are some pretty awful looking characters come in here. Take up a lot of time . . . "

"All right," said Johnny, "if I'm the lucky one, I'll have twenty dollars on Saturday."

"Are you kidding?"

"Not at all, Nancy; you're just about my size — "

"Stop right there, fella. I don't go out

with factory hands."

"Women," said Johnny, bitterly. "You'd go out with me if I were unemployed, but just because my hands are stained from honest toil — "

"Ixnay, ixnay," retorted Nancy Miller. "You were asking hypothetical questions and I was giving you hypothetical answers. I never said I'd go out with you, unemployed or working. My fiancé wouldn't like it . . . These are the men, Mr. Johnson . . . "

11

2

JOHNNY whirled. An elevator door nearby had opened and Johnson, the factory foreman, was coming toward them. He was a greying man of about fifty. He wore a tan linen smock. He stopped a few feet from Johnny and Sam and sized them up before speaking. Then he asked: "Which one of you boys came in first?"

"We came in together," Johnny replied quickly.

"The girl tell you what this job pays?"

"Thirty-two dollars a week."

"That's right. Time and a half for overtime." He made a clucking sound with his mouth. "I dunno, help ain't what it used to be. You fellows need jobs badly?"

"We must, if we're willing to work for thirty-two dollars a week."

Johnson grunted. "That's just it. You want a job because you need it, but will you work a couple of weeks until

12

something better comes along?"

Sam began to bob his head and Johnny himself almost fell into the trap. But he caught himself in time. "No, Mr. Johnson, we'd work right along. And we're not afraid of hard work. Sam used to be a wrestler one time. He can lift a barrel of leather with one hand. The job don't come too hard for Sam: Work all day and never get tired."

Judas, Sam's tortured eyes said to Johnny.

Johnson regarded Johnny steadily. "Sounds like you're trying to sell your friend for the job."

"No," Johnny replied. "I need the job as badly as Sam does, but we've been friends for years and we understand one another. Sometimes he gets the job, sometimes I do. There're things he can do better than I. If the job requires brawn and perseverance — "

"It doesn't," said Johnson. "You can sit all day long. It's sorting counters. Softest job in the place." He frowned. "As a matter of fact, the less imagination you've got the better you are for this job. That's why I think I'll take" — he looked

13

suddenly at Sam Cragg — "you!"

Sam took a quick step back, the color draining from his face. "Me?"

"Yes. What's your name, besides Sam?"

"Cragg," Sam said, hoarsely. "Sam Cragg."

"Good. Well, Sam, you can start right away . . . "

The girl at the switchboard suddenly called: "Mr. Johnson, Mr. Kessler wants to talk to you." She extended a telephone to Johnson.

Johnson took the telephone. "Yes, Karl, what is it? . . . What . . . ? All right, it's just as well. He's been nothing but a troublemaker, anyway." He slammed the receiver back on the hook, returned the phone to the girl, then whirled and stabbed a forefinger at Johnny.

"This is your lucky day, son! You and your friend don't have to split up, after all. One of my sorters just quit. That means there're two jobs open. I'm hiring you both. Come along . . . !"

Johnny reeled as if he had been struck by an invisible fist, but a happy, rejuvenated Sam caught his elbow and

14

helped him into the near-by elevator. Johnson followed them into the cubicle, closed the door and pulled a rope. The elevator shuddered, wheezed and began to groan its way slowly upwards.

Johnson surveyed his new employees. "Drifters," he said, "that's all working men are today. Go from job to job. Do as little work as possible. Always looking for an easier job and more pay. Social security, bah! Worst thing that ever hit this country. Me, I've never had but one job in my life. I started here when I was thirteen years old. Thirty-nine years and I've been a foreman since I was twenty-six. I've worked hard all my life and the company's treated me fine. I get two weeks vacation every year — with pay!"

The elevator stopped at the fifth floor and Johnson opened the corrugated iron door. "Well, here we are. I boss this whole floor. Ninety-two men — I mean, I mean sixty-four men and twenty-eight girls and women. Right through this row of barrels . . ."

Wooden barrels, one on top of the other to the height of four and almost reaching the concrete ceiling, were straight ahead of the elevator. Johnny was about to start between two rows, when a man entered at the far side and Johnny stood aside for him to come through, as the aisle wasn't wide enough for two people to pass.

The man was a hulking, beetle-browed man of about thirty. He carried a small package under his arm and wore a coat and hat. His face was set in a heavy scowl.

He came through the aisle, saw Johnson and spat on the floor. "The hell with you, Johnson, the hell with you and your job."

"All right, Carmella," Johnson said, calmly. "Pick up your pay, down in the office. I'm glad to get rid of you."

"And don't think I ain't glad to get the hell outta here," snarled Carmella, stepping into the elevator. He started to close the door, but held it open a few inches to deliver a parting shot. "And the hell with the Dook, too." He slammed the door shut.

Johnson shook his head. "Bad man. Shouldn't ever hired him in the first place."

"Is that the fellow whose job I'm

16

taking?" Johnny asked.

"Yes. And no matter how bad a worker you are, you couldn't be any worse than him. That's a relief, anyway." He drew a deep breath and started into the aisle between the barrels. Johnny and Sam followed.

The fifth floor of the leather factory was a vast place. It contained several hundred machines of various kinds, rows of long work benches, thousands of barrels containing leather findings and huge leather drying racks. Machines stamped and pounded, screamed and whined. It was a place of vast confusion and wonderful efficiency.

Leather came here, raw from the tanneries, huge, wrinkled, irregular sheets. Machines stamped out heels, counters, shankpieces, outer and inner soles. Other machines split the leather, trimmed and shaped it. Huge vats of glue soaked the leather, made it hard and tough, waterproof. Machines molded and shaped the pieces and at last they went into boxes and barrels and crates and were shipped to shoe factories all over the world.

No shoes were manufactured here, but

all the parts were made and sold to shoe factories which merely assembled the various pieces, sewed and nailed and merchandised the finished product as shoes. A leather counter went out at six or seven cents, a heel the same, a sole twelve or thirteen cents — all the parts necessary for a pair of shoes brought less than two dollars, but when assembled by the shoe manufacturer and placed in a store, they cost the consumer $9.95.

Johnson led Johnny and Sam to the rear of the great floor where a bench, fully a hundred feet long was set up against the wall. The bench was divided into sections nine or ten feet long and before each section a man sat on a high stool, sorting leather counters, those U-shaped pieces of leather that brace up the heels of shoes. Behind the benches, and suspended from the ceiling, were wire drying racks, each containing three or four hundred pairs of counters, molded wet from glue and wax the previous day by tremendous molding machines.

When the counters were sufficiently dry, they were dumped on the sorters' benches. It was the duty of each man to

18

sort the counters for heavy, medium or light grades, trim off imperfections with sharp leather knives and finally bunch the counters for packing. Four counters were nestled together, then inverted and pushed into another nest of four counters. These bunches were piled up on the bench and finally put into used sugar and apple barrels that held ten or twelve hundred pairs each. The barrels were covered with burlap, stenciled as to their contents, then either put into 'stock' or shipped to a shoe factory.

At the head of this long sorting bench, Johnson turned Johnny and Sam over to Karl Kessler, the assistant foreman, a middle-aged Austrian, who spoke with an accent.

"A couple of new men for you, Karl," Johnson said. He looked down the long bench. "Don't put them next to each other. They're pals and they'll gab all day long."

"Sure," agreed Kessler, "I see they don't talk."

Johnson walked off and Kessler looked brightly at Johnny and Sam. "All right, fellas, now we get to work, huh?" He stepped to a near-by section of bench that was unoccupied. Johnny and Sam followed.

He picked up a leather counter. "Know what these are?"

"Hunks of leather," Sam returned.

"Sure, that's right, they're counters, the things that hold up the backs of the heels. This bunch is 2 MOXO, that means Grade 2, Men's Oxford, Size 0. They're seven iron — "

"Iron?" asked Johnny.

"Leather thickness is measured by irons; forty-eight irons to an inch. Now, here's what you do. You sort these for heavy and medium, like this . . . " He smacked the counter into his left hand, squeezed it. "This is a heavy." He picked up another counter. "This one, too."

"If they're all seven iron," Johnny asked, "why aren't they all heavies?"

"Because no two pieces of leather are the same. Counters are cut from all around the hide; here's one from the shoulder, this one's a headpiece and here — here's the best of all, from the bend . . . "

"Bend?"

"That's a strip about a foot wide, over the back. Usually the soles are cut from there. Shoulder stock is next best. Worst is head stock; spotty, hard one piece, soft another. Ain't nothin' wasted on a cow, it's all used for somethin' . . . "

"What about the moo?" Johnny asked.

Kessler looked blankly at him. "The moo? What's that?"

"The moo from a cow." Johnny mooed.

Kessler laughed uproariously. "Ha ha, that's funny. Ha ha . . . " Then he broke off and grabbed up a counter. He slapped it into his left hand, caught up a knife and began trimming the flange on the counter. Johnny looking over his shoulder, saw a man bearing down on them, a tall heavy-set man in a blue serge suit.

"'Morning, Karl, 'morning," the big man greeted Kessler, cheerfully, as he approached.

Kessler looked up and pretended to see the man for the first time. He bobbed his head, actually bowed from the waist. "Good morning, Mr. Towner. Thank you, Mr. Towner . . . "

21

Mr. Towner stopped. "How's Elliott doing?"

"Fine, Mr. Towner, fine. Best counter sorter we've ever had."

"Glad to hear it. Don't favor him. Treat him just like anybody else . . . "

"Sure, Mr. Towner, sure. Thank you, Mr. Towner."

Mr. Towner smiled pleasantly and walked off. Kessler grabbed up a counter and fumbled it, from sheer nervousness. "That's Mr. Towner," he whispered. "The big boss."

"The guy who owns the works? Democratic, ain't he?"

"No, Republican."

Johnny, looking down the line, saw Mr. Towner stopping at one of the benches.

"That's his son, Elliott," Kessler whispered hoarsely. "Don't look at them."

Johnny picked up a leather counter, squeezed it. "You mean the old boy owns the joint and he makes his son work here?"

"Sure, Mr. Towner did that himself when he was learning the business. Old

Harry Towner started the company. When this Mr. Towner — Young Harry — graduated from college, the old man put him here in the factory — a week in every department, to learn how each piece of leather was made. Then he sent him out on the road as a salesman. Now Elliott's learning the business. We got him this week, next week he goes into the heel department. In three-four weeks he knows the whole business and starts selling."

Johnny shot a furtive glance down the line of benches. Young Elliott, a handsome young man, was wearing overalls, a tan work shirt and a cotton apron like the other counter sorters. His father was conversing jovially with him.

Johnny exhaled heavily. "Is he really the best counter sorter here?"

Karl Kessler gave him a quick look. "Are you kidding?"

Johnny chuckled. "Oh, like that, huh?"

"Comes in at ten o'clock, takes two hours for lunch. Goes to the club down on Michigan Avenue — "

"In that outfit?"

Kessler grunted. "Takes a half hour to wash and change his clothes. Young Harry wasn't like that. We used to work eleven hours a day in those days and Harry came in at seven in the morning like everybody else . . . "

"You were here then?" exclaimed Johnny.

"You kiddin'? I been here thirty-nine years . . . "

"Johnson said he started to work here thirty-nine years — "

"Yeah, that's right. He came to work about six months after I did. Just a punk. I broke him in. Used to kick him in the pants . . . "

"Still do it?"

"Huh? He's the foreman, now." Kessler risked a look off to the right, saw that Mr. Towner had left his son's bench and gone elsewhere. "All right," he said, to Johnny, "you can get to work here, now." He nodded to Sam Cragg. "You come with me."

He led Sam down the line to a vacant section of bench, adjoining that of Elliott Towner. Johnny shook his head and

24

picked up a counter. He squeezed it as Karl Kessler had shown him, put it down and squeezed a second counter. Not that the squeezing meant anything to him, but that seemed to be necessary.

3

A HISS at Johnny's left attracted his
attention. He turned and saw
a white-maned old man with a
white walrus mustache glaring at him.

"How you like the yob?" the oldster
whispered.

"Fine," Johnny replied, "just fine."

"Yah, I bet. No good, place like this,
for young people . . . "

"Oh, I dunno," Johnny said, easily.
"Sounds like a steady job to me. Johnson's
been here thirty-nine years and Kessler
says he came here before Johnson — "

"Yah, and you know how much money
Johnson gets?"

"Five hundred a week, I guess."

"He don't get five hundred a month.
Sixty dollars a week he gets and
Karl — t'irty-nine years he works
here and you know what he makes,
now? Forty-four dollars!"

Johnny whistled. "You make it sound
pretty bad."

26

"No place for young man. Fella like you should start himself a business. That's where the money is. Lookit the Dook — "

"The Dook?"

"Harry Towner, that's what they call him, The Leather Dook . . . "

"Oh, *Duke!*"

"Sure, Dook. One of the richest men in Chicago. Owns this place, four-five tanneries, stock in six-seven shoe companies, couple office buildings. His father died rich and the Dook he double the money. Few years the young Dook get it all . . . "

"The lad sortin' counters, down there?"

"Yah, young punk. Like have him on my ship for a voyage, I teach him few things. Don't know I'm old sea captain, huh? Yah, sailor all my life, until eight year ago, when they take away my ticket. Now I work in leather factory. 'Nother year or two and they fire me. Maybe I go back to Copenhagen."

Down the line, Sam Cragg had received his four or five minutes of instruction from Karl Kessler. The moment the assistant foreman left, Sam turned to Elliott Towner.

"What time do they bring the money around?" he demanded.

Elliott Towner looked at him pleasantly. "I don't think they bring any money around."

"The pay!"

"I'm sure, I don't know."

"You mean you're not interested," Sam snapped belligerently. "You're the boss's son, you don't care about your pay. You get your spendin' money whether you work or not."

"Oh, I say," protested young Towner. "That's a little unfair, isn't it?"

"Unfair, me eye! I get thirty-two bucks a week; how much do you get?"

"Twenty dollars."

Sam blinked. "Huh? Who're you tryin' to kid?"

"That's all they're paying me. And that's all I'll get until I start out as a salesman. Then I get raised to thirty dollars a week. Plus a small commission."

"Twenty bucks a week," snorted Sam. "That wouldn't pay for your lunches. You eat at your plushy club, don't you?"

"Yes, I do go down now and then. When I'm short of money. Of course I'm allowed to sign the tab at the club."

"Oh, so it comes out. You don't have to pay for your lunches. How about your duds? The old man pays your tailor, huh?"

"Naturally."

"Natcherly!" jeered Sam. "And you claim you're livin' on twenty bucks a week."

Young Towner's face was pale. "Now, look here, I think I've had about enough of that . . . "

"Oh, you're going to fire me, eh?"

"Of course not!" snapped Towner. "I can't fire anybody. I'm not the foreman. I'm a workman here, just like you. Not that I've seen you do any work . . . "

"A stool pigeon, huh? Spyin' on the workers. Snitch to the old man and get me fired. Beat down the poor workin' man, keep him starved, then kick him out when he can't work any more — "

"Is anybody *making* you work here?" flared Elliott Towner. "Did Johnson blackjack you on the street and *make* you take this job? You're a free man.

You can quit any time you like."

Sam opened his mouth to blast Towner, but just then Johnson, the foreman, came into the aisle from between a couple of rows of stacked-up barrels.

"You, Cragg!" he snapped. "You're a strong man; I've got a nice job for you, back here."

Sam shot a quick glance up the row of benches, saw Johnny Fletcher glaring at him and meekly followed the foreman through the rows of barrels.

Johnson led him to where a big swarthy man was wrestling a packed barrel of counters onto the platform of a portable elevator. "Here, Joe," he said to the swarthy man, "I've brought you a new helper. Let him do the cranking. That'll keep him out of trouble." He glowered at Sam and stalked off.

"Jeez," exclaimed Sam, "what is this — one of those sweat shops you hear about?"

The swarthy man looked furtively about, saw that no one else was within earshot, then said: "Take your time, small pay, small work." He picked up

30

an iron crank. "Here, you crank her. But no hurry, lots of time."

Sam, scowling, sized up the elevator. It consisted of a platform just large enough to hold a barrel and a steel frame, some eight feet tall. A steel cable wound up on a drum raised and lowered the platform, but for the raising it was necessary to insert the crank and turn it, until the desired height was reached.

Having set the barrel upon the platform, Joe stepped on himself. "All right," he said, "turn her over."

Sam inserted the crank in the proper place, began turning. It wasn't very hard work — not for Sam Cragg. The barrel weighed only a couple of hundred pounds or so and Joe's weight brought the total up to about four hundred pounds. Not too much, if you were as strong as Sam Cragg.

The elevator reached the height of three barrels. "Okay," Joe called down, "put on the brake . . . ."

"Yeah, sure," said Sam and pulled out the crank.

Only a quick leap backward saved him from a crushed foot, for the moment he pulled out the crank, the elevator platform dropped with a crash. Joe, fortunately, grabbed for the top of the elevator platform and now hung there, groaning and calling upon his saints in Italian.

"*Madre mio!*" he moaned. "He pull out the crank before he put on the brake." He let go of his grip and dropped to the floor of the elevator. Sam, seeing that the man was not hurt, stepped forward again.

"Why didn't you say I had to put the brake on first?" he growled.

"Even a fool would know that," snarled the Italian. "Anybody who's ever been around machinery knows what goes up, comes down, if you don't use a brake."

"I've never been around machinery," snapped Sam. "And you ask me, I'd just as soon not be around any now."

"Then why the hell don't you quit?"

"My pal won't let me. I didn't want to take the job in the first place, but he made me."

"There're plenty other jobs these days."

"I'd just as soon not work at all. I've

never had to before, not since I was a kid."

"You're a rich man, huh?" sneered Joe.

"No," said Sam, "I ain't rich, but look . . . " He suddenly stooped, upped the barrel that had crashed with the elevator, and hoisted it easily over his head. Stepping forward, he deposited it on top of a stack of three barrels.

"Gawd!" cried Joe. "That barrel weighs over two hundred pounds."

"To me it ain't no more'n a bag of peanuts," boasted Sam. "I'm the strongest man in the world."

"I wouldn't be a bit surprised if you were," conceded Joe in a tone of sudden respect.

"Let's stop foolin' around with this machine," Sam declared. "Just show me where you want the barrels piled and I'll pile 'em. I ain't had a good workout in a long time and maybe liftin' these barrels for an hour'll do me some good."

A half hour later, Johnson the foreman came to Johnny Fletcher as he was clumsily trying to put bunches of counters into a barrel.

"That friend of yours," Johnson said grimly, "is he a circus strong man?"

"We did a few weeks in a circus once, yes. Why . . . "

"He's back there lifting barrels of counters five and six feet up in the air."

"They only weigh a couple of hundred pounds, don't they?"

"Are you kidding?"

"No, Sam's the strongest man in the world."

"That's what he told me a few minutes ago. But — "

He broke off, for a sudden scream of horror rose above the noise of the thumping and pounding machines. It came from the direction of the stacks of barrels, where Sam was working. Johnny dropped a bunch of counters and rushed for the aisle leading to the rear of the barrels.

He hurtled through, reached a darkened area beyond. "Sam!" he cried. "Sam, are you all right?"

"Yeah, Johnny," came Sam's reply. "But come over here . . . "

Sam bounced out from behind a stack

34

of barrels some twenty feet away. Johnny rushed to him and collided with a shaking, swarthy man, Joe, who was staggering out of the aisle.

"His — his throat's cut," babbled Joe.

Johnny shoved the man aside, stepped into the narrow aisle between two rows of barrels. Halfway down, a stack of barrels had been removed and there in the narrow space, slumped down in a sitting posture, was a dead man.

4

IS eyes were wide and staring
and his throat had been cut
from ear to ear. Johnny took one
quick look and backed away. Johnson,
the foreman, standing at the end of
the aisle, peering in, cried out hoarsely,
"Who is it?"

"How should I know?" snapped Johnny.
He gestured. "You're the boss here, take
a look . . . "

A shudder ran through Johnson's body,
then he pulled himself together and
crowded into the aisle past Johnny.
He looked at the dead man's face and
gasped.

"Al Piper!"

"One of your boys?" Johnny asked.

"He runs a skiving machine." Johnson
swallowed hard. "He — he must have
committed suicide."

"Because he runs a — a, what did you
say? skiver machine?"

"Skiving. Uh, it isn't that, but Al, well,

36

he just got back to work today."

"Vacation?"

"You might call it that. Al takes one every six months."

"That's very nice of the company, giving vacations twice a year."

"The company doesn't give them. Al takes — took — them." Johnson inhaled deeply. "Al's a periodic boozer. Goes along for six months, then goes on a binge; usually lasts for a week or ten days, then he's all right for another six months." Johnson turned, found the eyes of Karl Kessler. "How long was Al gone this time?"

"Twelve days."

"Little longer'n usual. How'd he look?"

"Not bad. Little shaky, but not so bad, considerin'."

Johnson shook his head. "Guess it just got too much for him. He wasn't a bad guy, when he was working. He ran that skiving machine . . . mmm, must be eighteen or twenty years."

"Maybe that's why he did it," suggested Johnny.

Johnson's sharp eyes fixed themselves

upon Johnny. "The skiving machine's the easiest job on the floor, unless its sorting counters. He just sat there on a stool all day long, feeding flat counters into the skiver." He suddenly scowled. "What's the idea, all you people gawkin' around here? Get back to work."

The workers, who had been blocking the aisle, scattered swiftly. Even Johnny wandered off, but Sam remained. "Me, too?" he asked. "I was just gonna pile some barrels there . . ."

"They can wait. Get back to the sorting bench. I've got to report this to Mr. Towner."

He didn't think of the police. Mr. Towner was the highest authority in the leather factory and when something happened, you reported to him. But Towner must have notified the police for they came within fifteen minutes; a round half dozen of them, headed by Lieutenant Lindstrom of Homicide.

They searched among the stacks of barrels, set off a few flashlight bulbs, then began going through the counter floor, looking at machines, studying workers from concealed vantage spots and making them so nervous that a molding machine operator caught his thumb in the machine and lost about a sixteenth of an inch of flesh. After he went down to the first aid station, Lieutenant Lindstrom, escorted by Johnson the foreman, entered the counter sorting department.

They bore down upon Sam Cragg and began questioning him. Johnny, seeing his friend in difficulties, eased himself along the line of benches, carrying a couple of counters. As he came up, Lieutenant Lindstrom was just saying to Sam Cragg: "That's your story, but you can't prove that you never met Piper before today . . . "

"I didn't really meet him today," Sam retorted. "He was already dead when I saw him."

"Good for you, Sam," cut in Johnny.

Lieutenant Lindstrom whirled on Johnny. "Who're you?"

"Fletcher's the name, Johnny Fletcher."

"He's a pal of this man," explained Johnson. "I hired them together."

"As a team?"

"No — no, I just happened to need two men." Then Johnson suddenly grimaced.

"Say, I hired this one," indicating Johnny with his thumb, "to replace Carmella Vitali, who had just quit his job. Uh, Carmella and Piper had a fight about a month ago."

"About what?"

Johnson shrugged. "I wouldn't know, but Piper threw a handful of counters in Carmella's face and then Carmella beat up Piper."

"Beat him up, huh? And Carmella quit his job today when Piper came back after a vacation. Mmm," the lieutenant pursed up his lips. "I suppose you've got this Carmella's address?"

"Yeah, sure. I'll get it for you — "

"In a minute, Mr. Johnson." Lieutenant Lindstrom suddenly looked at Johnny. "Carmella told you he was quitting his job today, didn't he?"

Johnny grinned lazily. "You'll have to do better'n that to catch me, Inspector."

"Lieutenant!" snapped Lindstrom. His eyes glowed. "Sort of a wise guy, aren't you?"

"I get by. There was a sign outside the building, Man Wanted. Sam and I saw it and came in. Sam got hired, then

Mr. Johnson heard that this Carmella chap had just quit his job and decided to hire me, too. That's all I know about Carmella. Not one bit more, not one bit less. I never saw Al Piper. I never saw this factory before this morning." Johnny shot his cuffs back. "I've got nothing up my sleeves. Nor has Sam. You're wasting your time on us."

Lieutenant Lindstrom bared his teeth. "Get back to work."

But Johnny didn't have to get back to his work, just then. A tremendously loud bell rang on the counter floor and every man at the counter benches rushed for the aisles leading to the lockers beyond. Johnny, looking at a huge clock on the wall, saw that both hands had met under the figure twelve. It was lunchtime.

The workmen returned to the benches in a moment or two, carrying lunches, wrapped in newspapers. Lieutenant Lindstrom walked off with Johnson leaving Johnny and Sam alone.

Johnny, his tongue in his cheek, stepped up to young Elliott Towner, who was taking off his work apron. "How about joining us for lunch?"

"I was only going to run across the street to the lunchroom and have a sandwich," replied Elliott.

"A sandwich is okay with us."

Elliott looked at Sam, frowning. "Well, all right," he said, after a moment's hesitation.

"I worked up a nice appetite," said Sam, as they headed for the elevator. "Rassling them barrels. I think I'll have maybe two sandwiches and a glass of beer."

They rode down in the slow freight elevator. As they passed the office Johnny looked for Nancy Miller but failed to see her. He shook his head and followed Elliott Towner. Outside, they crossed the street and entered a grimy, smelly lunchroom. There were no stools at the counter, but it was lined with standing factory workers. The menu was a slate on the wall.

"Corned beef sandwich and a glass of milk," Elliott Towner ordered.

"Two corned beef sandwiches for me," said Johnny, "and a glass of beer."

"Same for me, on'y two beers," chimed in Sam.

The sandwiches were quickly prepared and Johnny and Sam began to wolf their food. They finished their double portions before Elliott Towner got through with his one sandwich.

"Piece of pie," Sam ordered then.

Johnny nodded. "Me, too. How about you, Elliott?"

"No, this will do me."

The waiter punched three checks, put them on the counter. Elliott sorted them out, picked up his own. A sudden chill ran through Johnny. A dollar-ten was punched on his check, the same on Sam's.

"Uh, Mr. Towner," he said, "I believe I'm a little short, on account of just starting work, you know. I wonder if you'd — "

Elliott Towner frowned at him. "Look here, you didn't come out to lunch with me, just to — "

"Oh no, not at all. Only we *are* short and — "

"How much are you short?"

"Well, my check's a dollar-ten and Sam's is, too. Two-twenty."

"That's the full amount. You've got

43

some money . . . "

"Not a red cent. Uh, you could take it out of our pay."

Young Towner exploded. "I tried to make it clear to your friend here that I didn't own the Towner Leather Company. I'm an employee like you. I get twenty dollars a week and I have to live on it."

"With a little help from the old man," Johnny said sarcastically, "and the chauffeur to bring you down to work."

"I've had about all I'm going to take from you two," Elliott said angrily. He started for the door, but Johnny gave a quick signal to Sam Cragg and the latter blocked his exit.

"Just a minute, buddy," Sam said truculently and put up a hand to stop Elliott. Elliott tried to knock the hand aside, was unable.

"Now, Elliott," Johnny said, smoothly, "look at it this way. We've got a tab here for two-twenty; we can't pay it. Are you going to let it get out that two employees of Towner and Company were unable to pay a restaurant bill and had to wash dishes all afternoon, while they were supposed to be sorting counters across the street?"

"You're not my responsibility," cried Elliott.

"Oh yes, we are," Johnny said, cheerfully. "Your name's Towner . . . "

"All right," snarled Elliott, "I'll pay your damn checks!" He grabbed them from Johnny's hand and stepped up to the cashier's desk. Johnny and Sam waited for him at the door.

As they left the restaurant, Johnny said, "No hard feelings."

Elliott gave him a glare and rushed across the street.

Sam Cragg exclaimed in disgust, "Never saw a guy like that. He's got a gold spoon in his mouth and he wouldn't even give you a sniff of it."

"Of course," said Johnny, "our act was pretty crude. I wouldn't have pulled it on him if I hadn't been so hungry."

"I'm still hungry," Sam complained. "I've got a lot of eating to catch up on." He screwed up his mouth. "What're we gonna do about supper?"

"We'll face supper when we come to

it. In the meantime we've got a couple of jobs on our hands."

"And a murder," Sam declared darkly. "For all you know, we may be spending the night in jail."

"Uh-uh," said Johnny. "Uh-uh."

5

THEY entered the leather factory and rode up to the fifth floor in the elevator. Wending their way back to the counter department, they discovered Lieutenant Lindstrom awaiting them at Johnny Fletcher's bench.

"Have a good lunch?" the lieutenant asked.

"It was all right," Johnny said, "not as good as we're used to, of course, but it was all right."

"Then you're all set for a nice afternoon's work."

Johnny looked sharply at the lieutenant. "You the foreman here now?"

"No, I just wanted to see you work."

"This is our lunchtime."

Hardly had he spoken the words than the bell rang and the counter sorters began streaming back to their benches. Johnny Fletcher picked up a counter, squeezed it and looked at the lieutenant.

"All right, I'm working."

47

"Go right ahead."

Johnny picked up a second counter, found that it was slightly imperfect and reached for the leather knife. It wasn't there.

"Looking for something?" asked the lieutenant.

"My knife."

"Isn't it around?"

"Cute," said Johnny. "You knew all the time it wasn't here; that's why you were hanging around. Well, it was here, when I went to lunch."

"It was here at twelve o'clock? But it isn't here now?"

"Al Piper was killed with a leather knife," Johnny said, "you think it's my knife. It isn't. Al was found a little after eleven. I was using my knife here until twelve o'clock. I can prove it." He turned to the old Dane, at the adjoining bench.

"Say, Pop, you saw me using my knife."

The old man scowled fiercely. "I didn't see nuttin'. I mind my own business. I don't know nuttin' 'bout nobody or nuttin'."

Lieutenant Lindstrom smiled wolfishly,

but Johnny wheeled to the man at his right, a faded, sandy-haired man of about forty.

"Neighbor, you saw me using my knife just before lunch?"

The sandy-haired counter sorter shrugged. "I was busy before lunch."

"Sure, sorting counters. But you don't keep your eyes on them all the time. You couldn't help but look over here now and then. I looked at you enough times."

"So I was thinkin'."

"I think, too," retorted Johnny. "But I see what people are doing around me."

"If you gotta know," the counter sorter said, coldly, "I was running down the horses in the sixth at Arlington. That takes concentration. Try it some time; past performances, post position, jockey, weight, condition of track. Do that sometime without a *Racing Form* in front of you and you'll know what I mean about concentration."

"All right," said Johnny, "who's going to win the sixth?"

"Fighting Frank. He can do it in 1:10 if he has to . . . "

"Not with a hundred and twenty-six

pounds," cried Lieutenant Lindstrom.

"He's done it before and he can do it again," insisted the counter sorter. "I got money says he can."

"Yeah? Well, I've got five on Greek Warrior in the same race."

"Greek Warrior's a seven-furlong runner; this race is only six furlongs. Ain't a horse at Arlington can beat Fighting Frank at six."

"What about Spy Song?"

"Phooey. An in and outer. All right when she was a two-year-old, but hasn't done a thing since."

"Good-bye, now," Johnny Fletcher said, walking back to his bench.

Lieutenant Lindstrom winced and followed Johnny. "We didn't settle the knife business."

"No, but you settled the horse business. You're interested in that, aren't you?"

"A wise guy. We get you downtown you won't be so smart."

"You take me down to the station you'd better have the answers," retorted Johnny.

"You talk pretty big for a factory hand," sneered Lindstrom.

50

"I haven't always been a factory hand," snapped Johnny. "Now, if you'll excuse me, I've got some counters to sort."

Lieutenant Lindstrom gave him a wicked look, hesitated, then whirled on his heel and strode off. Johnny gave his attention to the counters on his bench. He picked them up, squeezed them, trimmed one now and then and piled them up in bunches.

From time to time Johnny sent a look off to the right where Sam Cragg was at his bench, squeezing and bunching up counters. There was a big scowl of concentration on Sam's face, which did not lessen as the afternoon wore on. Sam was unhappy at his work.

Shortly after three Karl Kessler stopped at Johnny's bench.

"How you coming along?" he asked.

"It's a tough job," Johnny said, "all these decisions."

"Huh?"

"Every time I pick up a counter I've got to make a decision — is it heavy, medium or reject? Keeps your brain working."

Kessler looked at him suspiciously.

"Some fellas c'n do this in their sleep." He picked up one of Johnny's bunches of counters, opened it and tested each counter. "These are all right, for heavies."

"Heavies?" exclaimed Johnny. "Those are the mediums."

"Mediums? Where are the heavies?"

"The little pile in back."

Karl Kessler scooped up a bunch of counters from the rear of the bench, tested them individually and scowled. "How do you figure these are different from the mediums?"

"They're harder."

"Ah-h," grunted the assistant foreman in disgust. "These are all supposed to be heavies. They're seven iron, don't come much heavier. You shouldn't find more'n one medium out of twenty or thirty counters. Yours are running the other way." He hesitated. "Better sort 'em all over. Here, I show you . . . " He scooped back an armful of Johnny's 'mediums,' began resorting them. "Don't squeeze 'em too hard, you break down the glue. This is a heavy . . . and this . . . and this . . . "

52

"Guess I'm a little upset," Johnny said, lamely. "I don't usually run into a murder my first day on the job. That happen around here very often?"

Kessler shot a startled look at Johnny. "You kiddin'? Nothin' like that never happened around here."

"This Piper worked here a long time, didn't he?" Johnny asked.

"Not so long, sixteen-seventeen years. Can't figure it out, he wasn't a bad guy, drank a little too much, bet on the horses, but outside of that, he was a good family man . . ."

"He was married?"

"Oh sure, got three kids. I hear Mrs. Piper took it bad."

"Women usually do take it pretty bad when their husbands are murdered." Johnny paused. "Who's your choice for who did it?"

Kessler looked carefully around and dropped his voice to a whisper. "He had a fight with the guinea, didn't he?"

"Carmella?"

"Yeah, sure. You know these guineas, half of them belong to the Black Hand."

"The Black Hand! I haven't heard of

53

them in twenty years."

"Yah! This is Little Italy. The Death Corner's only three-four blocks from here. Oak and Milton. They used to kill people there all the time."

"How long ago?"

"Not so long. Twenty, twenty-five years ago."

Johnny shook his head. The assistant foreman's idea of time was out of this world. A man who'd worked at the factory fifteen years was a virtual beginner. He still used the pre-World War I epithet of 'guinea' for an Italian and the Black Hand, which had been extinct for twenty-five years, was still real in his mind.

The Towner Leather Company was Karl Kessler's life. He had worked for the firm thirty-nine years. Two great wars had been fought in that time. The American way of life had changed. Poor boys had become millionaires in that time. Children had grown up, married and become grandfathers.

Johnny said: "Is it your idea that the Black Hand's involved in this murder?"

"Who else? Carmella's a Blackhander and him and Al Piper had a fight."

54

"Carmella quit his job this morning; was that a result of the fight with Al Piper?"

Kessler frowned. "Well, maybe not exactly. Uh, he wasn't much good around here. Never sorted more'n fourteen hundred pairs a day and when I told him he'd have to hustle up . . . " He shrugged. "He got sore and quit."

"Fourteen hundred pairs a day," mused Johnny. "Seems like a lot of counters."

"Shucks, most of the fellas do two thousand pairs. Ain't nothin' for a man to do twenty-five, twenty-six hundred." Kessler gestured to Cliff Goff, the horse player. "How many pairs did you sort yesterday, Cliff?"

"Twenty-three hundred," replied Cliff Goff, "but it was a bad day. Hit some head leather seven and a half irons in the afternoon."

"That's bad?" Johnny asked.

"You'll see, head stock is spongy, uneven. You get a counter made of heavy head stock and it's like iron on one side and like mush on the other side. Here" — Kessler thrust his hand at the pile of counters — "look at this

55

piece. Beautiful piece of leather, ain't it? That's shoulder stock, smooth, even."

Johnson the foreman suddenly appeared from between two rows of barrels. He came up and halted between Johnny and Kessler. "How's he doing?" he asked the assistant.

"Pretty good for a beginner," replied Johnny.

"How many pairs have you sorted so far?" Johnson asked.

"About a thousand, I guess," Johnny said. "More or less."

"Less," suggested Kessler. "About six hundred less."

"That's not very many," Johnson said, "considering you've been at it since nine this morning."

"Don't forget we had a murder here."

"I'm not forgetting it," snapped Johnson. "But it'd be a good idea if *you* forgot it and thought more of your work. Remember, this is only your first day here."

He stalked off. Kessler hurried after him, talking and gesticulating with both hands. Johnny looked after them and began to wonder if his career at the

Towner Leather Company would be a very long one.

He slapped counters together, stood for awhile with feet planted far apart, climbed up on the high stool and took to standing again. His back ached from leaning over the bench and when he stood his feet hurt.

Four o'clock came and moved grudgingly to four-thirty. Sam Cragg deserted his bench and came over to Johnny. "We quit at five, Johnny," he said.

"Don't I know it? My neck's stiff from twisting it to look at the clock."

"Yeah, but what about some dough? We got to eat and get a place to sleep tonight. Don't you think we ought to get a — an advance on our pay?"

"You took the words right out of my mouth, Sam. Wait here."

Leaving Sam, Johnny headed out into the front part of the floor, where the row of molding machines were banging and pounding. He caught sight of the foreman just beyond, near the glue tanks.

"Mr. Johnson," he shouted to be heard above the din. "How's about getting a small advance on my pay?"

"Sorry, Fletcher," Johnson replied. "That's against the company's rules."

"But Sam and I are flat broke. We don't even have money for supper."

"You wouldn't have had it, if I hadn't given you this job, would you?"

"No, but we'd have taken it easy all day. We wouldn't have been as hungry as we are now, after exerting ourselves all day."

"You've got a point there," conceded Johnson, "but it's a rule of the company. You can't make exceptions."

"No, I guess you can't," said Johnny in disgust. He started to turn away, but Johnson called to him.

"Here, Fletcher." He thrust a hand into his pocket and brought out a crumpled dollar bill. "Here's a buck for you, from me, personally."

"Thanks, Mr. Johnson, that's mighty white of you." Johnny cleared his throat. "Uh, you wouldn't have another dollar, would you? Sam Cragg's pretty hungry, too."

Johnson swore. "Damn you, Fletcher!" But he brought out another dollar and handed it to Johnny. "Now, keep away from me so I don't change my mind and fire you instead."

Johnny returned to the counter department and handed Sam one of the dollar bills. "Buck apiece was all I could promote," he said.

Sam was disappointed. "I had my heart set on a steak and French fry dinner."

"So did I. Where's Elliott?"

"He beat it a couple of minutes ago. He's the boss's son, he don't have to wait for the whistle."

"Damn," exclaimed Johnny. "I was going to hook him for the steak dinners."

"After the way he acted this noon? I don't think even you could sell him on an encore."

"No? You underestimate me, Sam, when I'm desperate." His eyes suddenly narrowed. "Just a minute."

At the end of the line of counter benches was an old-fashioned bookkeeper's desk on which stood Johnson's telephone. Johnny strode to it and scooped the receiver off the hook.

"Nancy girl," he said into the mouthpiece. "This is me."

He heard her exclaim in astonishment. "Mr. Johnson . . . "

"Uh-uh, not the foreman," Johnny chuckled. "Give me a couple of weeks, will you . . . !"

"Fletcher!" she cried. "You want to get fired?"

"Not before I earn that twenty I need for Saturday. Look, Nancy, do me a favor . . . "

"I'm doing you one, now. Get off that phone! The workers aren't allowed to use the phone."

"Sure, sure, the regular workers, maybe. But I'm not a regular worker. But to cut a long story short, has Elliott Towner breezed through?"

"Yes, now will you — ?"

"Where does he live?"

"With his father — naturally."

"And where does the old man live?"

"Hillcrest."

Johnny winced. "That's way out in the country, isn't it?"

"About forty miles."

Johnny was about to hang up, but suddenly thought of something else. "What about Elliott's club?"

"The Lakeside Athletic on Michigan Avenue."

"That's it, Baby. Thanks a million. Remember Saturday . . . "

He hung up, started back toward Sam, but before he reached him the five o'clock bell rang and there was a mad rush for the sinks and lockers behind the rows of barrels. Johnny and Sam joined the stampede and had to wait in line to wash up.

"Do a good job, Sam," Johnny advised his friend.

6

AT ten minutes after five they left the leather factory and made their way to a near-by street corner. They clambered aboard a crowded streetcar and and fifteen minutes later alighted at Madison and Wells.

Johnny started to cross the street and Sam caught his arm. "Hey, you're going east."

"Certainly."

"Yeah, but we want to go west."

"West? That's where all the flophouses are."

"Ain't that what we're looking for?"

Johnny shook his head. "Sam, you've got ninety cents and I've got ninety cents. On West Madison we can find a joint where we can get a steak for that, but where'll we sleep — and what about breakfast in the morning?"

"I hadn't thought about that," admitted Sam. "But east of here, everything's more expensive."

"We're all washed up," Johnny said. "A little dust on our suits, but we don't look too bad." He cleared his throat. "I thought maybe we might have dinner at the Lakeside Athletic Club . . . "

"Huh?" Sam blinked, then reacted. "Not Elliott Towner?"

"Why not?"

"The way he acted this noon . . . "

"That was crude. I've had time to think now."

"All right, Johnny, he can't get any madder'n he is already."

"That's what I thought."

They walked swiftly down Madison and a few minutes later turned South on Michigan. The fourteen-story building housing the Lakeside Athletic Club was just ahead.

Johnny turned into the club door, Sam crowding at his heels. A uniformed doorman looked inquiringly at them.

"Yes?"

"We're going in to join Mr. Towner," Johnny said easily and would have gone through the inner door, except that the doorman moved a few inches and blocked his path.

63

"He's expecting you?"

"I rather think so."

The doorman reached to a high, narrow desk and scooped up a handful of slips of paper. He shuffled quickly through them. "There's no pass here."

"He probably forgot to leave one."

"I'll have to get an okay from him," the doorman said, picking up a phone. "Who shall I say is calling?"

"Mr. Fletcher and Mr. Cragg," gritted Johnny through his teeth.

"Michigan door, for Mr. Towner," the doorman said into the phone. "I believe he's in the steam room, now." He nodded, looked at Johnny and Sam. "Club rules, gentlemen. Hope you don't mind."

"Oh, we don't mind," said Johnny, pretending not to see Sam's warning signal.

The doorman turned back to his telephone. "Yes, Mr. Towner, Arthur, at the Michigan door. There's a Mr. Fletcher and Mr. Cragg here, say you're expecting them. No . . . ? . . . Just a moment, please." He covered the mouthpiece with a big hand. "Mr.

Towner says he doesn't know anyone named Fletcher and Cragg."

"We're from the plant," Johnny said. "Tell him that. It's important that we see him. Extremely important."

The doorman spoke into the phone. "They say it's an extremely urgent matter, Mr. Towner . . . Very well, sir . . . " He handed the phone to Johnny.

Drawing a quick, deep breath, Johnny said: "Mr. Towner, this is Johnny Fletcher . . . "

"And who the devil is Johnny Fletcher?" boomed the deep voice of Harry Towner.

"I'm from the factory," Johnny said, in desperation, "I — I have something very important to tell you about that — regarding what happened at the plant this morning."

There was a moment's pause, then Harry Towner grunted. "All right, give me Arthur."

Johnny handed the phone back to the doorman.

"Yes, Mr. Towner?" said the doorman. He bobbed his head. "Very well, sir. Thank you."

He hung up the phone, scribbled

65

quickly on a slip of paper and banged his palm on a bell on the desk. "Front!" he called.

A bellboy appeared from the lobby behind the little reception room. The doorman handed the slip to him. "Take these gentlemen to Mr. Towner in the steam room."

"This way," said the bellboy.

Johnny and Sam followed him into a large lobby, fitted out much like a hotel lobby. The bellboy headed swiftly for the elevators.

"Watch my cues," Johnny whispered to Sam Cragg as they followed the bellboy. "I asked for Towner and got the old Duke, instead of Elliott . . ."

"Holy cats!" exclaimed Sam.

"They can't do more'n throw us out."

They stepped into the elevator and were whisked up to the fourth floor where the bellboy led Johnny and Sam along a corridor and finally into a huge room, containing a fifty foot swimming pool and numerous steam rooms and cubicles where masseurs and attendants gave club members treatments.

The bellboy stopped a moment, looked

around and located Harry Towner. The Leather Duke was wearing a towel about his waist and nothing else. The bellboy headed for him.

"Mr. Towner, these are the gentlemen to see you," he said and went off.

Harry Towner searched the faces of Johnny and Sam, then shook his head. "You say you're from the plant? I don't place either of you."

"The counter department," Johnny said.

"That's Hal Johnson's floor."

"Our boss."

"You mean you're — you're *laborers*?"

Johnny pushed out his lips in a great pout, looked down at his hands, then suddenly looked up and beamed at The Leather Duke. "Shall we say we're working *as* laborers?"

Towner scowled. "What do you mean?"

"There was a murder at your plant today, wasn't there?"

Towner stabbed a nicely manicured forefinger at Johnny. "Now, don't tell me you're police undercover men?"

Johnny closed one eye. You couldn't exactly call it a wink, because he kept the lid down for a long moment. "Mr. Towner, there are some things I can't tell you — not at this moment. Shall we just say that — that we're working *as laborers* at your plant and that we, ah, have important information pertaining to what happened there this morning?"

"Now, wa — ait a minute," cried the leather man. "That plant happens to be my personal property. If there are any shenanigans going on there, I have a right to know . . . "

"Exactly, sir. And that's why we're here."

"Well, spill it, don't just stand there throwing *hints* at me."

"It'll take a little while to tell. Were you, ah, about to take a plunge?"

"I just had a steam and a rubdown. I intend to have my dinner and then . . . say, you can tell me this over dinner. I'll be dressed in just a minute. You've got the time?"

"We've got the time," said Johnny.

Harry Towner hurried off to a cubicle and Johnny and Sam exchanged significant glances. The ghost of a smile played over Johnny's lips.

68

"Dinner, Sam."

"Can you bull him through to the dessert, Johnny?" Sam asked, eagerly. "It must be two years since I've had any."

"The desserts at the Lakeside are the finest in Chicago," Johnny said. "I hope."

Harry Towner came out of the little cubicle in a few minutes, knotting a Brooks Brothers tie. "All right, gentlemen," he said, "we'll just run down to the grill room. A little quieter there than the main dining room."

"How's the grub?" Sam asked.

Towner looked at him sharply. "I beg your pardon?"

"The food, Mr. Towner," Johnny said, quickly. "Mr. Cragg is a bit of a gourmet, you might say."

"Yeah, you might say," said Sam Cragg.

"I like good food myself," Towner rumbled. "That's the only fault I find with the cuisine here — you can't get a good steak."

"You can't?" cried Sam.

Towner shook his head sadly. "They don't know enough to buy meat ahead.

69

A steak's got to hang for a couple of months or it's no good."

"You're absolutely right, Mr. Towner," enthused Johnny. "There's a little spot in Los Angeles, that is, in Santa Monica, down by the beach, where they really know how to cook a steak. They hang them in a cellar for three months, then scrape off the whiskers and put them on the fire . . . " Johnny rolled his eyes upwards. "That's a steak for you, sir!"

By this time the trio had descended a broad flight of stairs and entered a grill room that occupied about half of the entire third floor. Soft lights lit up each table and white-jacketed waiters moved smoothly in and out among the tables. A headwaiter led them to a table on a balcony raised a few feet above the main floor and brought them large menus.

Harry Towner looked at the card and shook his head. "You've given me an appetite for a steak, Mr. Fletcher," he said, sadly, "but they're simply impossible here. I believe I'll just have a watercress salad and a glass of skim milk."

"Oh, no!" groaned Sam.

Johnny said: "I'm a glutton for

punishment, Mr. Towner. I've said over and over, just how bad can a steak be? And I've said to myself, never again, but" — he smiled brightly — "I'll try once more." He looked up at the waiter. "I'll have a filet mignon and tell the chef to do his worst. Mr. Cragg, will you have the same?"

"With French fries," cried Sam, "and smothered in onions. And a big piece of apple pie — naw, make that apple pie à la mode. And all the trimmings with the dinner. I'm hungry."

"Why, Sam," Johnny chided, "you *are* hungry!" He laughed merrily. "So am I, for that matter. Do you know, Mr. Towner, we actually *worked* today. Gives you a terrible appetite when you're not used to it."

"Yes, I imagine so," conceded Towner. He placed his forearms upon the table and leaned forward. "And now, sir, if you'll tell me what's going on in my leather factory . . . "

"Ah yes," said Johnny.

"Yeah, Johnny," agreed Sam, "go ahead, tell him."

"Go right ahead, Mr. Fletcher. I'm not

one of these men who can't talk business while eating. You just tell me the whole story."

"Very well, sir, a horrible crime was committed in your factory today. A murder."

"Yes, yes, I know that. Go on, Fletcher."

"I'll have to bore you with a little background, Mr. Towner," Johnny said, "necessary background, so you'll understand the complete ramifications and meaning of this crime. You've heard of the *Mafia* . . . ?"

"The *Mafia*?" exclaimed Towner.

"The Black Hand, as it is commonly known in this country."

"But that's been dead for twenty-five years . . . "

"Has it, Mr. Towner? Let's just take a look back. A quick look. The *Mafia* originated on the Island of Sicily, about the same time that its counterpart, the *Camorra*, was being born on the mainland in Southern Italy. The *Mafia* was an outgrowth of the Napoleonic Wars. The large landowners could not operate their farms, so they turned the

72

work over to groups of ruffians, who by intimidations, threats and often violence, cowed other groups of ruffians, made them work the large estates. But soon the first group took things into their own hands. They rebelled against the landowners, put the squeeze on them and were soon the masters themselves. This was fine for the *Mafia*, but soon they were quarreling among themselves, one band of the *Mafia* against another. Many large bands were formed and all were at war with each other. They had only one law, in common to all of them, that was never to take their quarrels to the authorities. They were their own law, an eye for an eye, a tooth for a tooth. Absolute secrecy was enforced upon all members. Terrible reprisals were executed against those who talked. As the years went by the *Mafia* became powerful in all classes. Politicians feared them, joined them, The *Mafia* spread into Italy proper, into other countries. They became powerful in the United States in the nineties and in the early part of this century they ruled the Italian colonies in all the cities of this great country. Here in Chicago — "

"I know all about them," cut in Harry Towner. "I've lived in Chicago all my life."

"Right, sir. Well, your factory happens to be located in what is definitely an Italian section of the city, Sicilian, I should say — "

"It's called Little Italy, I know that."

"And you employ Italians."

"They make good factory hands, work reasonable and take orders. Much better than Germans or Irish, or even Bohemians . . . "

"But the *Mafia*, Mr. Towner, confines itself to its own kind — Italians."

"The *Mafia*," exclaimed The Leather Duke, "is extinct. It was smashed during the twenties, at the same time that its power was broken in Italy — yes, by Mussolini. That was the one good thing the man did . . . "

"The *Mafia* has been extinct before," Johnny said, somberly. "It was destroyed in 1830, or so the Sicilian authorities believed. It was wiped out in the 1860's and again around 1892, but always it came back. More furtive, more secret, more terrible . . . "

74

Harry Towner banged his fist upon the dinner table. "Are you trying to tell me, Fletcher, that the *Mafia* had a hand in the — the thing that happened today?"

"Mr. Towner," Johnny said, slowly, "I am not prepared to tell you that. It would be presumptuous of me to do so, at this stage. I'm merely telling you a little of the history of the organization, that's all, to show how it has always sprung up when it was least expected to do so. The *Mafia*, or Black Hand, as it is commonly called — "

He stopped. Two waiters were bearing down upon the table with huge trays of food. Harry Towner glowered at Johnny, then at Sam. He leaned back in his chair and watched while the servitors spread the plates around the table, the little plate containing his watercress salad and the large and numerous plates containing the viands ordered by Johnny and Sam.

7

THE waiters were still putting out food when Johnny and Sam attacked their steaks. Johnny munched a huge forkful of meat.

"You're right, Mr. Towner," he said, happily, "they simply don't know how to broil a steak here."

"Are you kidding?" cried Sam. He shoved half of a clover leaf roll into his mouth, pushed it back with about four ounces of steak.

The headwaiter came up to the table carrying an extension telephone. "Telephone, Mr. Towner." He plugged the cord into a socket.

"Who is it?"

"Miss Towner, sir."

The Leather Duke brightened, took the telephone. "Yes, my dear? . . . Oh, you are? Well, look, why don't you come down to the grill room? We've just started to eat. Fine." He put down the receiver. "My daughter's up in the main dining room," he said to Johnny. "They're coming down to join us."

"They?"

"Oh, she's with Elliott and her fiancé." Harry Towner made a careless brushing movement. "Continue, Fletcher, you were saying that the *Mafia* was behind this business."

"No sir," Johnny said, promptly, "I *didn't* say that. I merely reminded you that the *Mafia* has been considered extinct several times before and each time — "

"Damn this hush-hush stuff, Fletcher!" exclaimed Towner. "You're talking to *me* — you don't have to beat about the bush. You said that this man, what the devil was his name, Piper or Fifer . . . ?" He stopped, suddenly snapped his fingers. "You said yourself that the *Mafia* always confined itself to Italians. Piper is certainly not an Italian name."

"No, it isn't," said Johnny. "And that's exactly what I was driving at. This man *called* himself Piper — do you see, sir?"

The Leather Duke's eyes lit up. "Ah-h, yes!"

77

"We know, Mr. Towner," Johnny said softly, "that an Italian named Carmella Vitali had a quarrel with this man who called himself Piper and we know that Carmella quit his job this morning and that" — Johnny paused significantly — "shortly afterwards Piper was found dead, his throat cut!"

Harry Towner nodded thoughtfully. "The police took this Carmella into custody this afternoon: For questioning."

"They'll get nothing out of him," Johnny said promptly. "Nothing but evasions and lies. The rule of the *Mafia* — silence!"

"I'd make him talk," Towner said grimly. "If the police'd give him to me for a half hour, he'd talk. I'd take him and — "

He stopped, looked past Johnny and Sam. Johnny turned. Elliott Towner was approaching the table. Behind him was a tall, dark-haired man of about thirty, wearing tweeds, and the most beautiful girl Johnny had ever seen. She was fairly tall with dark chestnut hair. But it was her face that was really beautiful. Not that she had even, classical features, no,

78

many girls had those. This one had a sparkling vitality, a personality that jolted Johnny like a live power line.

He kicked back his chair, got to his feet.

Harry Towner also rose. "Elliott," he said, "Linda!" He put all the emphasis upon the girl's name. He ignored the fiancé completely.

"Dad," said Linda Towner and kissed her father on the cheek.

"Linda, Mr. Fletcher and Mr. Cragg."

"H'arya," said Sam.

Johnny smiled, leaned forward and she gave him her hand. "How do you do, Miss Towner."

She murmured an acknowledgment.

"My son, Elliott," went on Towner. Elliott stared coolly at Johnny. "We've met."

"Oh, of course, at the plant. Ah yes, I almost forgot. And, ah, Mr. Wendland, Mr. Fletcher, Mr. Cragg. We've been discussing business, but we're about through for the moment. Won't you sit down?"

A waiter brought additional chairs and everyone seated themselves. Johnny, aware that Elliott Towner was regarding him steadily, shifted his look from Linda Towner.

"You can't pay here," Elliott said.

Johnny looked at him blankly. "Eh?"

"Members sign."

Harry Towner heard the last remark. "What's that, Elliott?"

"Why, I was just saying that Mr. Fletcher and Mr. Cragg are fellow workers at the plant."

Harry Towner laughed jovially and slapped the table with an open palm. "So they are, Elliott, so they are, and you think — "

Johnny put a warning finger to his lips. "Mr. Towner, please!"

"But this is my family, Fletcher. Freddie, too — he's practically one of us . . ."

"Just the same," began Johnny.

"Nonsense, Fletcher, nonsense, I have no secrets from my family. They're interested in the business as much as I am."

"A secret!" exclaimed Linda Towner. "What is it?"

"A secret," said Johnny desperately.

80

Then Linda turned the full power of her hazel eyes on him. "A secret, Mr. Fletcher, connected with the business? And you're trying to keep it from me? You haven't got a chance. I'll get it from you, sooner or later, so you might as well save yourself wear and tear and spill it now."

Harry Towner sobered. "I don't know, Linda. It's rather unpleasant, but then you've probably already seen it in the papers . . ."

"Oh, that! Of course. As a matter of fact, Elliott was telling us about it upstairs." She suddenly turned to Sam. "Cragg — you're the Sam Cragg who found the body. Is it true that you lift up barrels of leather with one hand?"

"Naw," replied Sam, "I use two hands on account of its too hard to get hold of a barrel with one hand. But I could lift 'em with one hand if they had handles."

"What's that?" asked The Leather Duke.

Elliott turned to his father. "Sam Cragg's a strong man. He picks up two-hundred-pound barrels and raises them over his head."

Towner regarded Sam with interest. "You're really strong, eh?" He nodded in satisfaction. "Comes in handy with your work, I suppose."

"Yeah, sure," agreed Sam. "We don't have to bother cranking up that dinky elevator."

"Speaking of elevators," Johnny said loudly, "remember that Senegalese in Casablanca . . . " Then he winced. "No, I can't talk about that. Not yet."

"Why not, Mr. Fletcher?" Elliott Towner demanded.

Johnny squinted and looked at Harry Towner. The leather man took it up for Johnny. "That's the secret, Elliott. And perhaps Fletcher is right, the fewer who know the better . . . "

"The fewer who know what?" persisted Elliott.

Harry Towner hesitated and Johnny, with a sigh, put his napkin on the table. "What do you say, Sam, shall we get going?"

"Huh? I ain't had my dessert yet. I was figuring on apple pie à la mode. You promised me . . . "

"I know, but it's getting late and we've

82

got to stake out that place . . . "

"Stake out!" cried Linda Towner. "I know what that means. I read it in a detective story. Who're you going to watch, Mr. Fletcher?"

Johnny got to his feet. "I'm afraid I've said too much already, Miss Towner. You'll — you'll keep this quiet?"

"Of course, but . . . " She frowned in sudden thought. "I've half a mind to make you let us come along. Freddie, are you game?"

"Game for what, Linda?" asked Fred Wendland. "This is all a little too fast for me."

"How can you be so dense?" cried Linda. "What've we been talking about all through dinner?"

"Why, that horrible murder."

"And Mr. Fletcher and Mr. Cragg are going to do a stake-out. What does that suggest?"

"They're going to, ah, well what are they going to do?"

"I'm afraid we've got to run now," cut in Johnny.

Linda Towner got to her feet. "Wait — I'm going with you."

83

"Oh no," said Johnny quickly. "You couldn't possibly." He appealed to Linda's father. "Little Italy, hardly the place for — "

"Of course. Linda, sit down," said Harry Towner.

"I'm not afraid, Dad. It'll be fun — watching from a dark doorway . . . watching."

"I'm sorry, Miss Towner," Johnny insisted. "If it were possible, I'd let you come along. But it isn't."

Linda looked at him, sighed and seated herself. "All right, but I want to know all about it tomorrow. You'll tell me?"

"Yes," said Johnny, "I will."

"I'd like to hear it, too," chimed in Elliott Towner.

Johnny gave him a faint smile and tapped Sam's shoulder. "Come on, Sam. You'll excuse us . . . ?"

"I'll see you tomorrow, Fletcher," boomed Harry Towner.

Sam got up reluctantly from the table and followed Johnny. As they left the grill room, he said peevishly, "I can't understand why it is I never get around to the dessert. Somethin' always happens . . . "

"Something much more drastic would have happened if we'd stayed, Sam. Elliott doesn't like us one bit. We got a dinner out of it."

Sam brightened. "Such a line of bull, Johnny, I never heard."

"Every word I spoke was the truth, Sam."

"Huh? You told him we were undercover men."

"I told him nothing of the kind. Mr. Towner may have assumed from the *way* I spoke that we were more than laborers in his factory, but the words I used were true."

"Yeah, but that Black Hand stuff . . . "

"Nothing but the truth. I gave him a brief history of the *Mafia* and that was all. I told him that the *Mafia* had been extinct several times, which was true."

Sam thought that over until they had left the club and were turning the corner of Michigan into Madison. Then he exclaimed, "Yeah, but you said this guy Piper called himself Piper — "

"That's right, he did."

"He did what?"

85

"He called himself Piper because that was his name."

"The way you said it to the old boy it sounded like he was a — a Italian."

"Speaking of Italians, Sam, what do you say we take a little run over to Little Italy . . . ?"

Sam grabbed Johnny's arm. "No, Johnny, no, that's no place to go snooping around at night."

"Little Italy's no worse at night than any other place."

"But I know what you're figurin' on doing. I've seen it before. You're going to play detective and I'm going to get the hell beat out of me and we're going to wind up broke."

"We were broke this morning, Sam. Flat broke. Now, we've each got ninety cents in our pockets and we've had a couple of swell meals. But what about tomorrow?" Johnny shook his head. "We've no choice. Elliott's going to give us away to his old man. We'll have no jobs tomorrow, unless I can give the old man something to sink his teeth into."

"So we lose our jobs? What of it? We never had jobs before."

"But we had books to sell. We haven't got any now and we won't have until we get a stake. This job's got to give us that stake." Johnny hesitated. "And don't forget, *you* found the murdered man and *my* leather knife was missing from my bench."

Sam gasped. "You mean they — they suspect one of us?"

"And how! We're walking the streets free men, but suppose the cops decide that we're a couple of likely suspects, in view of the fact that they can't pin the rap on anyone else. What then? We can't *prove* we didn't kill Al Piper."

"But we never even knew the guy!"

"There are innocent men in jail right now," said Johnny ominously.

Sam groaned. "All right, Johnny, we'll go down to Little Italy. But I'm not going to like it. I'm not going to like it at all. Those Black Hands — "

"Don't be silly!"

They walked to Wells Street and in a few minutes caught a northbound streetcar. They got off at Oak Street and walked west in one of the worst slum areas in the city of Chicago. It was still early evening and there were plenty of people on the street, men, women and children.

8

THEY crossed Sedgwick and the houses became even more dilapidated. Paint had not been used in the neighborhood, it seemed, since the turn of the century.

Johnny walked carelessly, like a man out for an evening stroll, but beside him Sam walked on the balls of his feet, tense and uneasy. He glanced apprehensively at open doorways.

They reached Milton Street and Johnny said, "Oak and Milton, the Death Corner."

Sam shuddered. "Cut it out, Johnny!"

Johnny cleared his throat. "Kind of warm. A glass of beer wouldn't go bad."

"I'm not thirsty," said Sam.

"Well, I am. And here's a place — Tavern and Poolroom. Come on."

Sam groaned audibly but followed Johnny into the place, which turned out to be a long narrow room with a bar at the front and four pool tables in the rear.

They stepped up to the bar, which was quite well patronized.

"A short beer," Johnny said to the olive-complexioned bartender.

"Me, too," said Sam.

The bartender drew the beer, leveled off the foam and set the glasses before Sam and Johnny.

Johnny took a sip of the beer. "Carmella been around?" he asked, casually.

"That's twenty cents," the bartender snapped.

Johnny put two dimes on the bar. "I asked if Carmella had been around tonight?"

"Carmella who?"

"Carmella Vitali."

The bartender pointed to a frame on the back bar mirror. "There's my license for the bar," he said. He pointed to the wall behind Johnny. "And there's the one for the pool tables. There are no rooms in back and if anybody's betting on the games, they're doing it on their own. I just rent 'em the tables."

Johnny returned the man's truculent look with interest. "The hell with your

90

pool tables and your gambling. I merely asked you if a guy named Carmella Vitali's been around. I'm not a cop, if that's what's worrying you."

"So you ain't a cop, but I never saw you before an you come in asking for Carmella Somebody. I got a uncle named Carmella, but he can't be the guy you're looking for on account of he's been dead for twelve years and, anyway, he lived in Pittsburgh. He was born and raised in Pittsburgh and he died from gallopin' pneumonia."

Johnny gulped down the last of his beer and slammed the glass on the bar. "T'hell with you!" He signaled to Sam, who finished his beer and hurried after Johnny.

"What makes people so suspicious of everybody?" Johnny snarled as they resumed their walking down Oak Street.

"I dunno," said Sam, "but if somebody came around asking me about you, I'd figure they were after you for something."

"That's because somebody usually is after me, but all these people can't have somebody after them."

"Why not? Ain't somebody usually

after somebody for somethin'?"

Before Johnny could reply to that sage remark, a man stepped out of a doorway.

"Hey!" he cried, "what're you fellows doin' around here?"

It was Joe Genara, the swarthy man who had helped Sam Cragg pile up the barrels that morning at the Towner leather plant.

"Hiyah, Joe," Sam responded. "We're just takin' a walk."

"You live around here?"

"No," said Johnny, "but since we've taken a job in the neighborhood, we thought we'd look around and get acquainted."

"With this neighborhood?" Joe wrinkled his nose in disgust. "Phooey! Ain't nothin' around here worth seeing."

"Maybe not, but the people are interesting."

"You kidding?"

Johnny shrugged. "You've lived here all your life, you can't see that your people are colorful . . . Carmella lives around here, doesn't he?"

"Yeah, sure," agreed Joe, then looked

92

sharply at Johnny. "Carmella?"

"The lad the cops picked up for questioning about Al Piper."

Joe looked steadily at Johnny. "What're you driving at?"

"Nothing, only I'd like to meet Carmella."

"Why?"

"I got his job today. If he hadn't quit, I'd still be pounding the streets looking for work. I guess I owe Carmella a drink or two."

"I don't think he's in the mood to appreciate it, the way the cops gave him the one-two-three today."

"Maybe he needs cheering up."

Joe looked thoughtfully at Johnny, then glanced at Sam and a wicked grin spread over his features. "This might be fun, at that. I'll probably hate myself tomorrow, but — come on!"

He stepped to the curb and started across the street. Johnny and Sam followed. Joe led the way to a tavern and poolroom that was almost a twin of the one they had been in a few minutes ago.

Joe passed the bar and proceeded down

the line of pool tables. He stopped at the fourth and nodded to the last table.

"Go ahead, sports."

Carmella Vitali was just bending over the table. "Seven ball in the side pocket," he announced to an audience of four or five young men, all of whom had pool cues and stood around the table.

"Ten cents says you're crazy," one of the men exclaimed.

"Bet," said Carmella laconically.

He took careful aim and hit the cue ball with his cue. It struck the seven ball at the far rail and banked it neatly into the side pocket. The player who had made his bet banged his cue on the floor.

"Lucky shot!" He tossed a dime to the green covered table and Carmella pocketed it. He looked around the table, found the eight ball almost concealed behind the eleven ball.

"Dime you can't make it," said Johnny.

Carmella looked around, spied Johnny and scowled. "Private game."

"That's all right," said Johnny. "I'm not playing, but just the same I got a dime says *you* can't make that shot."

"I said this was a private game," Carmella repeated sharply.

"Sure, but you just took a bet on an easy shot; this one's harder. I got a dime says you can't make it."

Carmella's mouth twisted in anger, then his eyes took in the balls on the table. "Wise guy," he sneered. "I got a buck says you can't make that shot."

Johnny stepped forward, stooped and examined the balls closely. The eight ball could be hit all right, but if it was hit clean it would strike the twelve ball a few inches to the left. Of course, if it caromed off that ball just right, it would ricochet into the fifteen ball, which was blocking the corner pocket. No — not quite. The exact caroming from the fifteen ball could send the eight ball into the pocket. The shot was possible, but highly improbable.

Johnny straightened. "I think I'll just take that bet. Let me have your cue."

Carmella handed Johnny the cue, reached to the ball rack behind him and took down a piece of chalk. "All right, wise guy, make your shot."

Sam stepped up beside Johnny. "Ixnay, Johnny, you on'y got sixty cents."

"I know," Johnny said out of the corner of his mouth. "But you've got eighty. Besides. . . ."

He bent over the table, aimed carefully and hit the cue ball with his cue. The cue ball jumped sideways and Johnny recoiled in horror.

Then he lunged for the chalk that he had set down upon the edge of the table. Carmella was already reaching for it, but Johnny beat him to it. One glance told him.

"You've got soap in this chalk!" Johnny cried.

Carmella snickered. "Any soap in that chalk, you put it there yourself. You talked yourself into something and you figured that was an out. Only it ain't. A buck, mister."

"Put the cue ball back where it was and I'll try the shot again," Johnny snapped. "I didn't put that soap in the chalk, and you know it."

"Calling me a liar?" Carmella demanded truculently.

Johnny looked at the semicircle of

Carmella's friends. Their threatening looks told him that they were ready and willing to back up Carmella. But the dollar meant the difference between beds that night or sleeping in the railroad depots.

Johnny said: "I can make that shot."

"You didn't," snarled Carmella. "Now, give me that buck or so help me . . . "

Sam Cragg drew a deep breath and exhaled heavily. "Or what?" he asked.

"Who asked you to put in your two cents?"

"Nobody asked me," retorted Sam. "I'm puttin' in on my own. You outweigh Johnny thirty pounds. But I'm your size. You want to make something, pick on me."

"Belt him one, Carmella," suddenly urged one of Carmella's friends. "They're a couple pool hustlers."

"Yeah," agreed Carmella. "I seen 'em somewhere. Can't remember where, but they been around."

"You saw us at the Towner factory this morning," Johnny said. "As a matter of fact I got your job, after you were fired."

"Who was fired? I — " Carmella's eyes suddenly narrowed and he whirled and caught a pool cue from a rack. As he was turning back, Sam sprang forward. He whisked the pool cue from the Italian's hand, smashed it down against the table, snapping it in two.

"So you want to play rough," Sam cried. "All right, try this for size."

He hit Carmella on the side of the head with his open hand. The blow traveled only a foot or so, but it sent Carmella sprawling four feet, so that he collided with the first of his friends who was charging around the table to get at Sam and Johnny.

The blow was like a match set to a short fuse on a giant firecracker. Carmella's friends roared and came swarming forward. Two on one side, one around the other side of the table and a fourth over the table itself.

Pool cues flashed. Johnny took one pool cue on his raised forearm and cried out in pain. A second cue, poked at his eye, missed by an inch and cut open the skin over his cheekbone. Johnny jerked that cue away from the wielder

98

and without bothering to reverse, drove the heavy, leaded butt into the man's stomach, doubling him over and leaving him gasping in pain.

By that time Sam was engaged with his quota. He followed through on Carmella, grabbed him about the midriff and raising him clear slammed him into another man. Both went down to the floor. Sam hurdled them, caught another man in the crook of his arm and hugged him to his side. The victim belabored Sam with his fists and Sam hit him in the face, once. The man went limp, but Sam held him under his armpit. He turned, dragging the man with him to face Carmella and his ally getting up from the floor.

Sam whisked the unconscious man from under his arm, raised him to the height of his head and hurled him down on Carmella and his friend. The three men landed in a heap and did not get up.

Sam turned to go to Johnny's aid, found him exchanging blows. Johnny was doing fine, but Sam looked at the horde of men swarming to the rear of the room, from the other tables.

"Time to go, Johnny!" he cried. He ducked under Johnny's flailing arm, caught hold of his friend's antagonist and cuffing him with one hand scooped him up with the other. He raised him a good eighteen inches over his head, hurled him clear across a pool table in the general direction of the advancing crowd. The man took two or three others to the floor with him.

That was all there was to it. Johnny and Sam walked out of the poolroom without anyone else trying to molest them. And no one followed them out, not even Joe Genara.

On the sidewalk, they hurried to Milton, turned north and ran a block to Hobbie Street. There they scooted west and after a few minutes came out on Crosby Street. They walked quickly down Crosby and just as they reached Larrabee a streetcar came along. They boarded it.

The car had only a few passengers and Johnny and Sam had no trouble finding a seat. Johnny drew out a handkerchief and dabbed at the blood on his cheek.

"Kind of warm for a minute," he admitted.

"Oh, it wasn't bad," said Sam. "Best workout I've had for quite a spell." He grinned. "Little Italy isn't so tough."

"It was a waste of time, though — and money. Now we've got to find a place to sleep — for a dollar and twenty cents."

They got off the streetcar on Madison and began walking westward. Johnny studied the signs along the way. There were plenty of 'hotels,' advertising rooms at a dollar and cents. At Canal the prices began to come down and soon they saw signs advertising rooms as low as 35 cents, but Johnny was not satisfied with the appearances of the places.

"Flea bags," he said.

"As long as they've got beds, I don't care," Sam said. "If we're going to get up at dawn to go to work I want to hit the hay."

They reached Halsted Street and turned south and in the second block found a freshly painted sign, reading: "Private rooms, 30 cents."

"The sign's clean, anyway," said Johnny. "Let's bunk."

They entered a dimly lighted corridor

and the smell of disinfectant struck their nostrils. A flight of stairs led to the second floor and a small cubicle, containing a chair, a small bench and a grilled window in the wall. A frowsy old man was behind the grilled window.

"Got a couple of nice rooms?" Johnny asked. "For thirty cents?"

"Thirty apiece," was the reply. "Only one person to a room."

"That's us, kid." Johnny slipped thirty cents under the grill and Sam followed the example.

The man slipped an open book under the wicket. "Gotta register."

Johnny signed the names, Glen Taylor and Henry Wallace, and returned the book. The clerk looked at the names. "Again?" He yawned. "Okay. Rooms seven and eight, next floor."

"The sign said *private* rooms — where are the keys?" Johnny exclaimed.

"At the price we can't afford to lose keys. There's a bolt on the inside of every room. You can lock yourself in. But we ain't responsible for valuables."

"If we had valuables we wouldn't be staying here," Johnny retorted.

They climbed the stairs to the third floor and reached a narrow corridor, lighted by a single unshaded electric light bulb. On each side was a row of doors, some open, some closed. Johnny stepped to a door bearing the number seven.

Inside was an iron bedstead containing a mattress, an uncovered pillow and a ragged cotton pad. The room was one inch longer than the bed and two feet wider. It contained no other furnishings. The top of the cubicle was covered with chicken wire.

"Well," said Johnny, "it isn't the Palmer House, but I guess it's home, for tonight, anyway."

"Jeez," said Sam, morosely, "we eat dinner with a zillionaire at the Lakeside Athletic Club and then we bed down at a dump like this."

Johnny exhaled wearily. "Who knows? Maybe tomorrow night we'll sleep out at Towner's home. A good night to you, Sam."

He stepped into Room 7, groped for the light switch and found there was none. Johnny swore under his breath, slammed the door shut and shot the shaky bolt. Then he threw himself upon the bed without even taking off his shoes.

He was asleep in five minutes.

9

A MAN came along the corridor in the morning and banged on the doors. "Rise and shine," he roared. "Seven o'clock."

Johnny groaned and sat up on the bed. He blinked and shook his head to clear away the sleep. Then he saw where he was and got to his feet. He opened the door and stepped out into the hall, to meet Sam just coming out of his own room.

"Hey, you!" roared Sam at the man banging on the doors. "What's the idea, waking people in the middle of the night?"

"Everybody's got to be out by eight o'clock or pay extra," the man retorted.

"We've got to be at work by eight, Sam," exclaimed Johnny. "Come on." They hurried to the rear of the corridor where a sign over a door, said: Lavatory.

Inside was a galvanized iron washtub and a couple of long grey towels, hanging

105

from a nail. Being already dressed they had the edge on the other guests of the hotel and were washed before anyone else came into the room. The late risers would find the towels slightly soiled and rather wet.

They left the hotel and walked to Madison. Turning east, they found a restaurant where for fifteen cents apiece they had oatmeal, two stale rolls and coffee. That left them thirty cents, but Johnny decided that they ought to keep a small stake and they walked the two miles to the Towner leather factory, arriving there at three minutes to eight.

The office was deserted, those employees apparently not coming to work until nine o'clock. And the elevator was not running, so they were compelled to climb to the fifth floor.

They were just entering the counter department when the eight o'clock bell rang. All the counter sorters were at their benches, with one exception, Elliott Towner.

Joe Genara came up, grinning. "Hi, fellas, enjoy our neighborhood last night?"

"Where'd you disappear to?" Johnny

asked suspiciously.

"I watched it from the sidelines. Wasn't my fight. If I were you I wouldn't go walking around Oak and Milton tonight. Carmella and his gang are ready for you." He winked at Sam Cragg. "Nice exhibition, Sam."

"I didn't even get warmed up," said Sam.

Hal Johnson came into the sorting department from between two rows of barrels. "Break it up," he snapped. "The bell rang five minutes ago."

Genara scurried to his bench and Sam went off, scowling. Johnny grabbed up a couple of counters but Johnson remained at his side. "You're a disturbing influence, Fletcher," he said. "I'm beginning to think I made the mistake of my life hiring you. Who hit you in the face?"

Johnny touched the broken skin on his cheek.

"Had a little trouble with the Black Hand last night."

"The Black Hand! Are you crazy?"

"The *Mafia* . . . "

Johnson made an angry gesture. "Don't tell me about the *Mafia*, I grew up in this neighborhood. There hasn't been any *Mafia* . . . " He stopped, looked suspiciously at Johnny. "You been listening to Karl Kessler?"

"He did mention something about the Black Hand."

Johnson snorted in disgust. "Karl's got the Black Hand on the brain. Every time an Italian gets into an argument or a fight, he sees the Black Hand." He shook his head. "I don't know what you're doing, working in a factory, Fletcher, but you look like a man with a fair amount of intelligence . . . "

"Thanks, boss!"

"Ah-h-rr!"

Johnson made an impatient brushing motion and walked off. Chuckling, Johnny began to sort counters.

Ten minutes later, Karl Kessler, his face red, came up beside Johnny and began to look over his bunched counters. "What's the idea tellin' Hal Johnson I said the Black Hand killed Al Piper?" he demanded.

"Johnson told you I said that?" Johnny asked, in surprise.

"He said you told him I was talking

about the Black Hand."

"Well, you were, yesterday."

"But I didn't say the Black Hand killed Al Piper. Al wasn't a guinea and guineas only kill guineas in the Black Hand."

"Look, Karl," said Johnny, patiently, "Johnson came along and asked me who gave me this mouse on the face and I said the Black Hand, that's all. It was a joke, like some fellows would say they bumped into a door when they got a black eye."

Kessler examined Johnny's face with interest. "Who smacked you?"

"A guy," said Johnny. "I stuck my nose into his business."

"Yeah, that's what you get for sticking your nose into somebody else's business."

"I just said that."

"So you did and it's a good thing to remember." Karl pushed back a nest of counters. "These are okay for mediums."

Johnny was about to say that the counters were heavies, but Karl Kessler trotted off and Johnny moved the bunch of counters over to the medium side.

He sorted a few counters, then became aware that Swensen, the old Dane, was casting furtive glances his way. "Ahoy, mate," Johnny called to him.

"No yob for a young man," the old sea dog said, shaking his head. "Should start a business. No future workin' with your hands. Kessler, Johnson, thirty-nine years one yob. They never see the world. Me, I have been in Rome, Cairo, Sydney, Shanghai — "

"And now you're workin' here."

"I get beached. Unlucky, but I have seen the world. I got memories."

"So have I," said Johnny.

"What memories young fellow have?"

"I'm the world's greatest book salesman," said Johnny, cheerfully. "I've made fifty thousand dollars a year. One year I made more money than the President of the United States."

"Yah!" jeered Swenson, "and I am Lord Nelson one time."

"Okay," said Johnny, "you have your dreams and I'll have mine. I don't suppose you'd believe that I had dinner with Mr. Towner last night, yes, The Leather Duke himself."

"Yah," snorted Swenson. "I'm thinking you're world's biggest liar!"

Hal Johnson came striding from the direction of his desk, his face as dark as a thunderhead. "Fletcher," he cried. "I just got a phone call from the office . . . Mr. Harry Towner wants you to come right down."

Johnny nodded casually. "Thanks, boss." He winked at Swensen, whose mouth had fallen open.

"What's it all about?" cried Johnson.

"Tell you later," said Johnny easily, "mustn't keep Harry waiting, you know."

Johnson struck his forehead with his open palm and leaned against Johnny's desk for support. He watched Johnny walk off.

Johnny rode down to the first floor in the elevator and approached Nancy Miller's desk. "'Morning, Taffy," he greeted her. "Where'll I find Harry?"

"Harry?" gasped Nancy. "Have you gone completely goofy?"

"Not at all, Taffy, Harry wants to see me."

"*Mister* Towner?"

"That's right, The Duke himself. Guess he wants to ask me a few things about the leather business. I told him last night at the club that he ought to make a few changes around here and — "

Elliott Towner came out of an office, some twenty feet away. "Fletcher!" he called. "Here."

"Ah, the young Duke," exclaimed Johnny. "See you later, Taffy."

He breezed past Nancy's desk and headed for Elliott Towner. "How're you this morning, El?" Johnny asked as he came up.

"*I'm* fine," Elliott replied grimly. "But I don't know how *you'll* feel in a few minutes." He stepped aside so that Johnny could enter The Leather Duke's office.

It was a big room, some twenty-four by thirty feet in size. It had a rug about three inches thick and some hand-carved teakwood furniture. Harry Towner sat behind an enormous desk, a fat cigar in his mouth. Elliott came into the office behind Johnny and closed the door.

"Mr. Fletcher," began Harry Towner, "I see you've a bruise on your face this morning. Something go wrong with your little stake-out last night?"

"Oh, nothing much, Mr. Towner,"

112

replied Johnny easily. "Hardly worth mentioning. Six or seven men attacked Cragg and me, but it didn't amount to much."

"No, I don't suppose so, since there were only six or seven. But let's get to the point, Fletcher; about this *Mafia* business . . . "

"Yes?"

Harry Towner puffed mightily on his cigar three or four times, sending out clouds of smoke that should have warned Johnny. "I want a short answer, Fletcher, a yes or a no, if it's possible for you to use those words. Are you, or are you not, an undercover man?"

"Why, Mr. Towner," exclaimed Johnny. "Whoever gave you the idea that I was an undercover man? I'm a counter sorter here at this factory. I'm employed up on the fifth floor — "

"Yes or no!" roared The Leather Duke.

"Yes," said Johnny.

"Yes, what? You're an undercover man?"

"No. Yes, I'm a counter sorter."

Towner took the cigar from his mouth

113

and laid it carefully on the edge of an ash tray. He placed his hands flat on his desk. "Now, answer the next question briefly, not with a yes or no, but briefly. Why did you come to see me at the club last night?"

"Why, I didn't come to see you, sir. Sam and I went to the club to call on Mr. Elliott and the doorman happened to phone you. I had asked for Mr. Towner, and — "

"I'm trying to be patient, Fletcher," Harry Towner said thickly. "So answer me *briefly* — please! Why did you want to see Elliott?"

"Because of one of your company rules, Mr. Towner."

The Leather Duke pressed down hard on the top of his desk with his hands. "There's a company rule about calling at the Lakeside Club . . . ?"

"Oh, no, that isn't what I meant. There's a company rule about giving employees an advance on their salaries. You see, Sam and I are stony and since Mr. Elliott was kind enough to buy us our lunches yesterday, we thought, well — "

114

"No!" whispered Harry Towner. "No, no, no!"

"Yes," said Johnny. "We came to the club for one reason only, to get Mr. Elliott to buy us our dinners."

"It's true, Dad," exclaimed Elliott Towner. "They practically invited me to have lunch with them yesterday, then when the checks came they insisted I pay for them. Made quite a scene at the little place across the street."

"No, no," said Johnny, "that wasn't a scene. I merely pointed out that it wouldn't be good company policy to allow a couple of Towner employees to spend all afternoon washing dishes, inasmuch as — "

"Fletcher," said The Leather Duke, "that business about the Black Hand . . . "

"Words, Mr. Towner. To keep your mind occupied until the dinners came. But I told you only the truth, sir. About the Black Hand and — about us. I said we were working here as laborers. We are. I gave you a history of the Black Hand, a true history. If you misunderstood . . . "

Harry Towner suddenly pushed back

his big chair and got to his feet. "Wait, Fletcher. Be still for ten seconds. Don't say another word."

He turned his back to Johnny and smacked his right fist into the palm of his left hand. Johnny looked at Elliott Towner, smiled weakly. The Leather Duke's son gave him a bleak look in return.

10

FOR thirty seconds the only sound in the room was the heavy breathing of The Leather Duke. Then he turned.

"That story you just told me about how you got that bruise, Fletcher . . . "

"The truth, sir. After we left you last night, Sam and I rode up to Little Italy; we went into a poolroom and I got into an argument with Carmella. He and four or five of his friends attacked us. As a matter of fact, I can prove that. There was a witness, a man who works up in the counter department . . . "

"His name?"

"Joe Genara."

Harry Towner stabbed at his son with a forefinger. "Go upstairs, Elliott. Ask this Genara man — "

"All right, Dad," said Elliott. He started for the door, but as he opened it, Towner called, "Wait!"

He turned back to Johnny. "You'd let

him go up and ask?"

"Of course, sir."

"All right, Elliott," Towner said, "never mind." He drew a deep breath. "All right, Fletcher, let's have it. Why are you here?"

"Why, you asked me to come down and — "

"There you go with your words again," Towner snapped. "You know very well that wasn't what I meant. Why are you working here at this factory?"

"Because I'm broke. Actually, I'm a book salesman."

"A salesman!"

"The world's greatest and I'm not bragging when I say that, Mr. Towner."

"No, I don't think you are. You certainly sold me last night." Towner picked up his cigar and puffed on it. "A salesman, eh?" He suddenly flicked a switch on an interoffice communication system and leaning over his desk, barked out: "Come in here, Edgar!" He shut off the intercom and looked thoughtfully at Johnny.

"I've always prided myself upon being a judge of character," he said to Johnny.

118

"I thought I had you sized up last night, but if I've made a mistake . . . "

He stopped as the door opened and a completely bald man came into the room.

"Mr. Bracken, our sales manager. Edgar, this is Mr. Fletcher, one of our counter sorters."

At the beginning of Towner's introduction, Mr. Bracken came forward, hand out, a smile on his face, but at the final announcement of Johnny's status the smile disappeared from his face, the hand fell and Mr. Bracken came to a halt.

"Yes, Mr. Towner," he said, puzzled.

"Mr. Fletcher," Towner went on, "tells me he's a salesman. I'm going to give him a try out. I want you to give him some counter samples and an order blank. He's going to call on the John B. Croft Shoe Company and get an order for some counters . . . "

"The John B. Croft Company!" exclaimed Mr. Bracken. "But, Mr. Towner, you know — "

"Yes, I know," cut in Towner, "they buy lots of counters. They make a poor grade of shoes, but still they use counters

119

in them and we sell counters. All grades and all prices. Well, Fletcher, do you think you can get an order of counters?"

"And if I sell them?"

Harry Towner shrugged. "You won't be working upstairs."

Johnny grimaced. "Has this company ever sold the John B. Croft Shoe Company any counters?"

"Oh, yes!"

"How long ago?"

"How long is it, Mr. Bracken?"

The sales manager gulped. "Uh, twelve years."

"I see," said Johnny. He drew a deep breath. "Give me the samples."

Mr. Bracken looked at Harry Towner. The Leather Duke nodded grimly. "Give him the samples, Mr. Bracken. And the order blanks."

"And a small expense account, Mr. Towner," Johnny said. "I haven't even got carfare."

"Oh, you won't need carfare, Fletcher. They're only a few blocks from here. But you're right, a little expense money is only fair. Bracken, give him ten dollars . . . You're going to call on them now, Fletcher?"

"Yes."

"Good. I'll be waiting here to find out how you made out."

Bracken started to leave the office and Johnny followed. As he passed Elliott he heard a distinct snicker.

Bracken led Johnny into a small office near Towner's. When Johnny had entered the sales manager closed the door.

"I don't know what this is all about, Fletcher," he said, "but I feel that I should tell you that there is great enmity between the John B. Croft Company and this firm . . . "

"Oh, sure, I gathered that."

"John B. Croft has a standing order in his place that anyone from the Towner Company should be thrown out the moment they set foot in their factory. You'd only be wasting time calling there. If you're wise you'll take the ten dollars in lieu of your salary here — "

"I'll take the samples, too. And the order blanks."

Bracken looked at Johnny a moment, then shaking his head, went to a long table and picked up a leather salesman's kit. He handed it to Johnny.

"It's your funeral."

Johnny opened the kit, took out two leather counters and stuffed them into his pocket. He picked up an order pad and tore off two sheets, which he folded and put into his breast pocket. "Now if you'll give me the expense money . . . ."

Mr. Bracken took out his wallet and extracted a ten dollar bill. "Good-bye, Fletcher," he said.

"See you in a little while," Johnny said. He gave the sales manager a half salute and left the office.

He stopped at Nancy Miller's desk.

"Fired?" she asked.

"Promoted. I'm now a salesman. I'm going over to get an order from the John B. Croft Company."

She gasped. "Somebody's ribbing you."

"The Duke. He says if I get an order from Croft I can have any job in the place."

"But that's it, Johnny," Nancy said, tautly. "You *can't* get an order from the Croft Company. Harry Towner and John B. Croft are deadly enemies."

"I'm doing it because of you, Taffy,"

Johnny said, dramatically. "You said you wouldn't go out with a laborer, so I'm trying to become a white collar man, a salesman, just so you — "

"You're crazy, Johnny," Nancy said, softly. "Crazy, but I like you. Only — "

"I shall return," said Johnny, and walked out of the office.

But out on the street, some of his confidence ebbed from him. He walked north to Division Street and turned east. At the corner of Larrabee, he stopped for five minutes and had almost decided to give it up when his eye caught a sign over a store on the other side of the street. ASSISTANCE LEAGUE.

On a sudden impulse he crossed the street and entered the store. On the inside it looked like an orderly junk shop. Secondhand clothing in all stages of wear and tear hung from racks. Rusted tools and hardware were spread out on counters. Near the rear of the shop was a counter piled high with old shoes. In front of the counter stood four wooden barrels, all filled with old shoes.

A thin, pale man who looked like a reformed boozer blocked Johnny's path.

"Something for you?"

"Shoes," Johnny said. "Size nine and a half."

The clerk pointed at one of the counters. "Here you are, but we don't guarantee the sizes."

"Good enough, I'll guess."

Ten minutes later Johnny showed the attendant two objects that had once been shoes. The uppers were cracked and worn, the toe of one shoe had a half inch split and the soles of both had become loosened. In one there was hole clear through.

"How much?" Johnny asked.

The attendant had the grace to blush. "Why, ah, where did you find those?"

"In the barrel. Not very good, are they?"

"We're supposed to sort them out before we put them on sale," said the clerk. "We make it a rule to sell only wearable merchandise."

"Do you think these are wearable?"

"Well, I suppose there's *some* wear in them . . ."

"Look," said Johnny. He took hold of the sole of one of the shoes, yanked suddenly and ripped it halfway down. "Is it wearable now?"

"No, but you — "

"I know," cut in Johnny. "But what would you say they were worth before I did?"

"I'm supposed to get fifty cents a pair, but — "

"That's a deal," said Johnny, "if you'll wrap them up — in a newspaper . . . "

The clerk wrapped them and then there was some difficulty about making change for the ten dollar bill, but it was finally managed by going next door to the drugstore. At length, Johnny was back on Division Street, with a newspaper-wrapped parcel under his arm.

He crossed Milton and looked apprehensively off to the right in the direction of Oak Street a couple of blocks away, but continued on up Division. A few minutes later he came to the plant of the John B. Croft Shoe Company, a modern six-story brick building. He entered.

The reception room was lined with pine paneling and had a nice pine desk in one corner behind which sat an attractive redheaded girl. Two men were seated in

125

leather armchairs, apparently awaiting the pleasure of Croft executives.

"Mr. Croft," Johnny said to the receptionist. "John B."

"You have an appointment?"

"No," said Johnny. "I have no appointment."

"Mr. Croft *never* sees anyone without an appointment."

"Tell him that Mr. Fletcher is calling."

"You're a personal friend?"

"No."

"Then I'm afraid it wouldn't be of any use for me to tell him. Mr. Croft never sees anyone without an appointment."

"Tell him that Mr. Fletcher wants to see him."

"If you could tell me the nature of your business . . . "

"Personal."

"But you just said that you didn't know him."

"I don't, but my business is personal. Tell him . . . "

The redhead winced and picked up her phone. "Just a moment, I'll see if his secretary will see you . . . " She spoke into her phone: "Miss Williams,

126

there's a man here insists on seeing Mr. Croft. He says it's personal and . . . yes, I know, but could you come out?" She hung up. "Miss Williams will be out."

Miss Williams came presently. She was short and stout and wore a pince-nez. "You want to see Mr. Croft?" she asked, loftily. "What is it about?"

"I told this beautiful redheaded young lady that my business with Mr. Croft was personal."

"I'm Mr. Croft's confidential secretary. I can't interrupt him unless you tell me the nature of your business."

Johnny said, firmly: "You know all about Mr. Croft's affairs, eh? Well, just go in and tell him that Mr. Fletcher is here and wants to see him. Fletcher. F-l-e-t-c-h-e-r. Just tell him Fletcher and tell him to think hard. And tell him I'll wait three minutes. No more. Got that, girlie? The name is Fletcher and I'll wait three minutes."

The confidential secretary looked at Johnny, startled, then realized that she was wasting precious seconds and hurried off. She returned in two minutes and forty-five seconds. She held open the door.

"Will you come in, please?"

Johnny went down a wide hall, into a reception room at the end. The stout secretary hurried up from behind him and opened a paneled door.

Johnny went in.

John B. Croft's office was as large as Harry Towner's, but instead of teakwood, he favored dark mahogany. He was a little man — little, fat and balding. He was perspiring lightly.

"You wanted to see me, Mr. Fletcher?" he asked, a bit nervously.

Johnny nodded, crossed the room and sat down in a leather-covered chair some five feet from the shoe manufacturer. He placed the newspaper parcel carefully on his lap and looked at John B. Croft.

John B. Croft cleared his throat, coughed and cleared his throat a second time. "I, ah, I'm afraid I can't place you, Mr. ah, Fletcher, isn't it?"

"Fletcher," said Johnny.

Mr. Croft concentrated hard and his face showed a little more perspiration. "What is, ah, the nature — I mean, what did you want to see me about?"

Johnny waited about thirty seconds, then said quietly: "You've got a very nice business here, Mr. Croft."

Mr. Croft wiped his forehead with the back of a pudgy hand. "Shall we, ah, uh, come to the point, Mr. Fletcher? I don't imagine you came here to talk about the shoe business."

Johnny pursed up his lips into a great pout and held it a moment. Then he carefully picked up the parcel from his lap and broke the string. He folded the string and put it in his pocket. Mr. Croft's eyes were glued upon the package.

Johnny opened the paper cautiously, picked up one of the ancient, battered shoes, then the other. He rose from his chair, stepped to Mr. Croft's desk and placed the shoes carefully upon it. The shoe manufacturer stared at the shoes a long moment, looked at Johnny, then back at the shoes and finally again at Johnny. There was an inquiry in his eyes.

"Shoes," said Johnny.

Croft ran the tip of his tongue about

his lips. "I — I don't understand."

"Look at them."

Croft reached out a hand, hesitated, then touched one of the shoes gingerly. Since it didn't explode in his face, he picked up the shoe and stared at it. He shot a look at Johnny, then looked back at the shoe. He touched the sole that was pulled away from the uppers and then suddenly switched the shoe around and looked at the inside of the heel.

"A Croft," he said, tentatively.

"A Croft shoe," agreed Johnny.

A drop of perspiration fell from Mr. Croft's face to the back of his hand, causing him to twitch.

"Feel the counters," suggested Johnny.

Mr. Croft felt them. "Broken down."

"Pretty badly," agreed Johnny.

"I — I don't get the point," said Croft, nervously.

Johnny reached into his side pocket and bringing out his two sample counters, placed them carefully beside the battered wrecks of Croft shoes.

"Counters," he said.

Mr. Croft put down the shoe, picked up the counters. He felt them, looked questioningly at Johnny. Johnny pursed up his lips again.

"You never heard my name, Mr. Croft?" he asked, quietly.

"N-no, no, I don't think so. At least I can't remember. I — I have a bad memory for names and faces."

"I guess you have, Mr. Croft." Johnny took the order blanks from his pocket, unfolded them and carefully removed the creases. Then he spread the blanks out on Mr. Croft's desk. Mr. Croft took one startled look at them and returned his gaze to Johnny's face.

Johnny nodded slowly. "I'd like to sell you some counters, Mr. Croft."

"Harry Towner," Croft whispered.

"I beg your pardon?"

"How many?" exclaimed Croft, flicking sweat from his face, with a shaking hand.

"Oh, about ten barrels of 2 MOXO and . . . " Johnny hesitated, "say, ten barrels of 2 MOXOO . . . Could I use your pen?"

"S–sure . . . "

Johnny got up, took Mr. Croft's ball pen from the desk set and wrote out the order. He handed the pen to Croft. "Now, if you'll just sign."

Croft signed his name eagerly and handed the pen back to Johnny. Johnny returned it to the pen stand. He folded up the order blank.

"Thank you, Mr. Croft."

"Uh, th — thank you, Mr. Fletcher." Then, as Johnny started for the door. "What about these . . . shoes?"

Johnny looked back and smiled faintly. "Oh, that's all right, Mr. Croft. There won't be any trouble . . . *now* . . ." He smiled again and opened the door.

In the outer office, he nodded gravely to Miss Williams and walked through.

When he reached the sidewalk it was Johnny's turn to perspire.

11

IT was five minutes to twelve when Johnny re-entered the offices of the Towner Leather Company. Nancy Miller gasped when she saw him.

"You came back!"

"Of course. I said I'd return, didn't I?"

"But it's all around the office — Mr. Towner sent you out on an impossible mission . . . "

"Impossible?" asked Johnny. "I don't know the meaning of the word."

"But you were going to call at the John B. Croft."

"I went," said Johnny. "I saw Croft. I got an order."

"No!"

"Yes! Now, stick around, Taffy, and when I come out of The Duke's office, I'll have some good news for you — about our date." Johnny winked at Nancy and strode to Edgar Bracken's office. He stuck in his head.

133

"Edgar!"

Bracken looked up from his work, his eyes widening in shock. Johnny crooked a finger at him. "Come, Ed!"

He strode to Harry Towner's office and without knocking, pushed open the door. Towner was just hanging up his telephone receiver.

"Fletcher!" he exclaimed, unbelievingly. "What in the devil . . . ?"

Bracken padded into the room behind Johnny, came to a halt, just within the door, ready for instant flight. Johnny strode across the room, drawing out the Croft order.

"Salesman Fletcher reporting, Mr. Towner!" He unfolded the order blank and held it so that Towner could look at it.

Towner kicked back his chair, sprang to his feet and tore the order from Johnny's hand. "Twenty barrels!" he roared. "Where'd you get this?"

"From the Croft Shoe Company — naturally. That's John B. Croft's signature . . . "

"It's a forgery!"

"Mr. Towner!" Johnny said, indignantly.

"This is another of your stunts, but you're not going to get away with it. You think I won't call Croft."

"Go right ahead, sir."

Towner regarded Johnny suspiciously. "This order is genuine?"

"Of course it is. Mr. Croft signed it himself. A little, fat, bald-headed guy."

"That's Croft, all right. But . . ." Towner's eyes slitted. "How did you get it?"

"Why, I just went into his office and asked him for an order for counters and he gave it to me. That's all there was to it . . ."

Towner grabbed up his telephone. "Get me John B. Croft," he snarled.

Johnny strolled to one of the chairs and seated himself carelessly. Then Croft was on the wire. "Croft," snapped Harry Towner. "I have an order here for twenty barrels of counters, signed by you . . . What . . . You *did* sign it? . . . What's that? . . . I don't know what the hell you're talking about, Croft. The same to you, in spades!" He listened for a moment, his eyes screwed up in a frown. "You signed the order? That's all I wanted to know. You'll get the counters and you'll pay for them, too!" He slammed the receiver back on the prongs and looked ominously at Fletcher.

"What really happened, Fletcher?" he asked, slowly. "The truth . . . "

"The truth, Mr. Towner. I asked to see Mr. Croft and when I got into his office I asked him — "

"Croft mumbled something about an old pair of shoes and . . . blackmail."

"Blackmail? I don't know what he's talking about . . . " Johnny suddenly grinned. "All right, Mr. Towner, the truth. I stopped in at a secondhand store on Division. I bought the worst-looking pair of Croft shoes I could find. Props. They gave me the appointment business at Croft's office. I scared the hell out of them. Not by what I said, but the way I said it. Significant pauses, emphasis upon my name. I told Croft's secretary I'd wait three minutes, no more. Perfectly true; if he wouldn't see me in three minutes, he wouldn't see me at all. Croft saw me. I went into his office and sat down and let him carry the ball. He's got a guilty conscience — most men have, you know. At one time or another they've taken out a little lady they oughtn't to have taken out. Or something. So I just sat there and let Croft get himself all worked up. Then I opened the package containing the shoes and let him look at them. Then I showed him two of our counters and asked him if he wanted to buy some. I could have made out the order for a hundred barrels, but I let him off easy. Of course, if you insist I'll go back and get the other eighty barrels . . . "

"No," said Towner, thickly. "It won't be necessary. You proved your point. You're a salesman."

"I told you I was."

"So you did. You sold John Croft, but you've sold a tougher man than he, you sold *me*. You passed the test. I'm not going to say a word about your methods. I gave you an impossible assignment and you proved that it wasn't impossible. I guess your methods were justified. Now — the reward. Name it, Fletcher . . . !"

Johnny looked thoughtfully at his hands, then shifted his glance to Edgar Bracken. The little sales manager cringed visibly. "How much does your job pay, Mr. Bracken?"

"S–seven thousand a year," stammered the sales manager.

Lieutenant Lindstrom appeared in the office door behind Bracken. "Excuse me, gentlemen," he began, then saw Johnny and scowled. "You, Fletcher, just the man I want to see."

"Here we go again!" sighed Johnny.

"What is it, Lieutenant?" demanded Harry Towner, impatiently. "More questions?"

Lieutenant Lindstrom drew a notebook from his pocket. "Last night, at eight-forty-three this man and his big friend entered a poolroom on Oak Street. They got into a quarrel with Carmella Vitali and started a riot . . . "

"I know about that, Lieutenant," said the Leather Duke. "He told me."

Lindstrom's eyes narrowed. "I had a man shadowing Carmella. What I want to know is — why did you go there last night?"

"I wanted to pump him," said Johnny.

"About what?"

"Now, look, Lieutenant, let's not

be cute. There was a murder here yesterday . . . ”

“I haven't forgotten it,” Lindstrom said, grimly. “Nor have I forgotten that your leather knife was missing And I haven't forgotten the coincidence of your starting to work here the morning of a murder and your poking your nose into Carmella's business . . . ”

“Lieutenant,” said Johnny, drawing a deep breath. “Do you know *who* murdered Al Piper?”

“I don't at this minute, but — ”

“Do you know *why* he was killed?”

“No, but — ”

“You don't know, Lieutenant,” Johnny interrupted. “And *I* don't know. But I think I'll know before you do.” He turned to Harry Towner. “Mr. Towner, this affair isn't helping the business any, is it?”

“Our stock dropped four points this morning,” snapped Towner. “I want this mess cleaned up as quickly as possible. I mean that, Lieutenant. I talked to the mayor a half hour ago . . . ”

“I know you did, Mr. Towner. I got a call from Headquarters ten minutes ago.

But you've got to co-operate with the police, Mr. Towner. You can't protect your employees, just because — "

"I'm not protecting anyone," Towner said, curtly. "You get proof that someone committed this crime and you'll find me backing you, to the last dollar I've got."

"I may hold you to that," the lieutenant said stiffly and walked out. As he left the office he had to step aside for someone who came swinging in.

Linda Towner.

"Dad," she said, then saw Johnny. "Mr. Fletcher, I was hoping to run into you. I thought perhaps you could talk me into buying your lunch."

Johnny grinned. "There's been a slight change in my situation since last night."

"Oh, you talked Dad out of firing you? I was tempted to make a bet with Dad that you would, but then you see I know him so much better than I know you . . . "

"Be quiet a minute, Linda," growled Harry Towner. "I have a discussion to conclude with Mr. Fletcher." Towner cleared his throat noisily and glared at Edgar Bracken. "You say you want

140

Bracken's job, Fletcher?"

"Me? I wouldn't touch it. A sales manager sits in his office all day. I wouldn't like that."

"The counter sorters sit at a bench all day," said Towner. "Although sometimes they stand."

Out in the factory, bells rang signaling the lunch hour.

"Excuse me a moment," Johnny exclaimed and left the office. He strode to Nancy Miller's desk, handed her a couple of dollars. "I'm in a big conference, Taffy," he said, "but hand this money to my pal, Sam Cragg, as he comes out. Tell him to have a good lunch and I'll see him afterwards . . . "

"Conference with the duchess?" asked Nancy.

"The Duke. I've already turned down the sales manager's job."

"You're kidding!"

"Uh-uh, I'm going to get something bigger. Tell you about it later."

He patted her shoulder and returned to Towner's office. In his absence, Edgar Bracken had slipped out.

"All right, Fletcher," said Harry Towner.

"What job do you consider better than the sales manager's?"

"Factory detective. I want to devote my full time to finding the murderer of Al Piper."

"But the police will take care of that," protested Towner.

"Maybe they will," said Johnny, "and maybe they won't. They've got a lot of cases to solve. Besides, they're police and people clam up when a policeman's around. Me, I'm one of the boys, a counter sorter like the rest of them. I've an unusual knack of stirring things up."

"So I've noticed," offered Linda Towner. "That's one of the reasons I like you."

"Linda!" exclaimed her father.

Johnny chuckled. "Why don't we talk it over at lunch?"

"Can't," said Harry Towner. "I'm having lunch at the club with some of the directors of my tannery."

"Well, I'm not," declared Linda. "*I'm* having lunch at the Fluttering Duck."

"That's a coincidence," exclaimed Johnny. "I was planning to have lunch

142

at the Fluttering Duck myself. That is, I was going to have lunch there if I settled this little business with Mr. Towner."

"It's settled," said Towner. "I think you're making a mistake turning down the sales manager's job, but perhaps we can talk about that again, after this mess is cleared up." He grunted. "I have an idea you'll do as well as the police."

"I won't do any worse." Johnny coughed gently. "It's customary for a detective to get a retainer. Five hundred, shall we say . . . ?"

"Five hundred!" cried Harry Towner.

"And say, another five hundred when I hand you the murderer."

Harry Towner opened his mouth to blast Johnny, but suddenly shook his head and reached for his wallet. "All right, that order you got amounted to around three thousand. A five hundred dollar commission isn't too much."

"The order is for free," said Johnny, "you're paying me for detective work."

"Call it anything you like. Here's your money."

He handed Johnny four one hundred dollar bills and two fifties.

"My car's outside," said Linda Towner.

Nancy Miller had apparently gone out to lunch, for her desk was vacant. Johnny was just as glad that she did not see him leaving with Linda Towner.

Parked at the curb, in the only available space — in front of a fire hydrant — stood a canary yellow convertible Cadillac.

"You drive?" Linda asked Johnny.

"Only jalopies," replied Johnny. "Those fenders are too big for me."

She got in behind the wheel and Johnny climbed in beside her. She started in second gear and by the time she reached the next corner was doing forty-five.

"That wild story you told Dad last night," Linda said, "was that really just to get a free dinner?"

"Yes and no. We needed the dinner, but more than that I needed to sell myself to your father. One day of sorting counters was about enough."

Linda laughed. "Dad didn't want to believe it, even after Elliott told him

144

what you had done to him at lunch. And now you talked Dad into believing you're a detective."

"It so happens that that's one thing I'm good at," Johnny declared. "For instance, did you know that the man in the black Chevvie's having an awful time keeping up with us?"

Linda started to look over her shoulder, but Johnny exclaimed, "No — don't. Look in the rear vision mirror."

Linda followed his order. "There's a black coupe behind us, all right, but what makes you think it's following us?"

"Turn left at the next corner."

Linda gunned the motor of the Cadillac, then made a left turn that caused the tires to screech. Johnny, looking in the mirror, saw the black Chevrolet careen wildly as it almost missed the turn.

"Now make a complete turn around the block and get us back on Larrabee," Johnny said. "If he's still with us then, he's following."

Three minutes later they were back at their starting point and the black Chevrolet was seventy feet behind them.

"Okay," said Johnny, "he's following us."

"I can lose him," cried Linda.

"What's the good of that? Then I'd only worry about him. Continue on to the Fluttering Duck."

12

TEN minutes later Johnny and Linda got out on Wabash, turning the yellow Cadillac over to the doorman of the Fluttering Duck. The black Chevrolet was double-parked a short distance away.

They entered the restaurant and the headwaiter immediately escorted them to a table.

"I'll have a dry Martini," Linda said, as they were seated.

"Beer for me," said Johnny.

"Beer!"

He grinned. "I'm a working man. By the way, are you sure you didn't have a lunch date today with Freddie?"

"Why, no. And if you don't mind I'd just as soon not talk about him."

"Well," said Johnny, "we don't have to talk about him, but I'm afraid you're going to have to talk *to* him, because here he is."

Fred Wendland, his hair nicely

147

pomaded, was bearing down on them. His face had a sullen, unhappy expression.

"Linda," he said, "I thought I might run into you here."

"Oh, did you?" Linda asked coolly.

Wendland pulled out a chair. "D'you mind?"

"Yes," said Johnny.

Wendland had not even looked at Johnny so far and if he heard him he gave no sign. He sat down. "I called your home and the butler told me you'd gone into town with your father. It's about tomorrow night, the fraternity's asked the alumni to a housewarming, for the new house and I thought — "

"Which team are you on?" Johnny asked. "Fraternity or Alumni?"

Wendland turned deliberately and looked at and through Johnny. "Oh, hello, Fancher, isn't it?"

"Fletcher."

"Ah yes, Fletcher. From the tannery, aren't you?"

"The factory, son. And ten'll get you twenty that you get sore before I do."

"I'm afraid I don't follow you."

"For example, what business are you

going into after you get out of school?"

"Stop it, Johnny," said Linda. "Fred's been out eight or nine years."

"But he was just talking about his fraternity house . . . "

"He's an alumnus and you know it very well. Let's have a more or less peaceful lunch, shall we? I'm hungry."

"You order for me," Johnny said, "I want to have a little chat with the man from the black Chevvie."

"He's come in?"

"Little table, just inside the door."

Johnny got up and crossed the room. He pulled out a chair opposite the man who had followed them to the Fluttering Duck. He was a rather insignificant-looking man of indeterminate age, but probably in his late thirties.

"Mr. Smith, I believe," Johnny said.

"I beg your pardon!"

"Aren't you John Smith of Keokuk, Iowa?"

The man shook his head. "You've made a mistake."

"Oh, I don't think so," said Johnny easily. "Let me see, you drive a black Chevrolet coupe, License 7 S 57-08 . . . My name is Johnny Fletcher, I work for the Towner Leather Company, and the young lady with me is the boss's daughter, Linda. The fellow with the shiny hair who just broke in on us is Freddie Wendland, her fiancé. Next question?"

"If you don't mind," the insignificant looking man said, "I don't know what you're talking about. I just stopped in here to have my lunch . . . "

"Who put you on my tail?"

"Tail? I don't think — "

"You don't think you know what I'm talking about. Never heard of Al Piper either, did you?"

"Wasn't a man by that name, ah, murdered yesterday?"

"Right!" cried Johnny, "and for that you win the jackpot, and the mink coat, and the furnished house and lot and the table model electric refrigerator, plus a ten year's supply of Royal Snus snuff. And would you like to try now for the sixty-four dollar question?"

"Got a big mouth, haven't you?" the man across the table asked, "and I see somebody bopped you one recently . . . "

"Last night, on Oak near Milton.

150

Didn't happen to see it?"

"No, but if you play a return engagement, let me know and I'll make it a point to be there."

"Oh, you'll be there, all right. That's your job, isn't it? To follow me."

"You're doing all the talking."

"You've done a little yourself."

The man signaled a waiter. When the latter came over, he said: "I'd like a bacon and tomato sandwich on toast. Plenty of mayonnaise . . . "

"Mayonnaise," said Johnny in disgust, and getting up returned to his own table.

As Johnny seated himself, Linda leaned eagerly across the table. "What did you find out?"

"I found out that he isn't as smart as he thinks he is," Johnny said, grimly. He reached into his pocket and brought out his four hundreds and two fifties. He peeled off one of the fifties and caught the eye of their waiter who was hovering nearby.

"Could you get me change for this?" Johnny asked. "Say four tens and a couple of fives."

"Yes, sir!"

"Oh — and by the way, your doorman checked in a black Chevrolet coupe a few minutes ago. License 7 S 57-08. Could you get me the name and address of the owner?"

"Why, yes, I believe I could," said the waiter. He moved off swiftly with the fifty dollar bill.

Johnny looked brightly at Linda. "Now, where were we?"

"You and Freddie were exchanging insults," said Linda, "but we decided to stop that and listen to you make like a detective."

"That's right," said Johnny. "The first thing a good detective does is to check on the alibis of all persons connected with the crime. Let's begin with you, Linda. Where were you yesterday morning?"

Linda started to laugh, then realizing that Johnny was regarding her seriously, she sobered. "Now, surely, you don't think *I* had any connection with that?"

"It's your father's factory."

"You mean you also suspect Dad?"

"Everyone connected with the plant is a suspect, five hundred people, more or less. There's only one of them I don't suspect — myself."

"But that policeman suspects you quite strongly."

"True. But *I* know I didn't do it, so I can eliminate myself."

"And you can eliminate me. I wasn't anywhere near the factory yesterday."

"Check!" Johnny shifted to Wendland. "And you?"

Wendland drew back. "Are you insane, man?" he gasped. "This — this man who was killed was a common laborer."

"So?"

"I'm afraid I don't move in such circles."

Johnny's eyes smoldered as he studied Wendland. "That's a very good idea, Mr. Wendland. Associate with working people and you might pick up their habits, such as going to work yourself."

"What he means, Freddie darling," put in Linda, "is that you're a stuffed shirt and a snob. Or to put it more succinctly, a stinker."

"You took the words right out of my mouth," said Johnny.

Fred Wendland pushed back his chair and got to his feet. "Very well, Linda, if you're going to side with him . . . "

"Run along, Freddie."

"I'll phone you tonight."

"Do that. Perhaps I'll be home."

Wendland bowed to Linda, gave Johnny a frigid look and walked off.

"You know," said Johnny, "I don't think Freddie likes me."

The waiter moved up to the table. "Here's your change, sir," he said, unctuously, counting out the bills one by one, four tens, two fives. "The party didn't have an ownership card in the car, but the manager has a book in his office which gives the name and address of every car owner in the state — "

"And . . . ?"

"The black Chevrolet, License 7 S 57-08 is registered in the name of Wiggins Detective Agency . . . "

"I'll be damned," exclaimed Johnny.

The waiter coughed gently. "Your change, sir. Four tens and, ah, two fives . . . "

"Ah, yes, thank you." Johnny picked up the bills, riffled them together and stowed them into his pocket. The waiter groaned and went off.

154

"He'll probably put his thumb in the soup," Johnny said, "so I think we'd better skip that course . . . Wiggins Detective Agency. Now, who the devil would be hiring a detective agency?"

"Why don't you ask the man?"

"Linda," said Johnny, "you ought to be a detective yourself. Excuse me a minute."

He got up and crossed the room. The insignificant-looking private detective was taking a bite of his bacon and tomato sandwich when Johnny came up. He stopped halfway through the bite, with the sandwich in his mouth.

"Who's paying the Wiggins Agency to have me shadowed?" Johnny demanded.

Mayonnaise dripped through the fingers of the private detective. He became aware of it after a moment and removed the sandwich from his mouth. He picked up his napkin and wiped the mayonnaise from his fingers.

"Sorry. Never heard of the Wiggins Agency."

"Your car's registered in the Wiggins Agency's name."

"How did you . . . ?" The detective

caught himself, scowled at Johnny. "Beat it, fella, you're spoiling my lunch."

"I hope so. Anybody who'd eat mayonnaise . . . " Johnny shrugged and walked back to his table. The waiter was putting out the food, setting down the plates with a little more than necessary annoyance.

"He won't talk," said Johnny, "but I've got him worried."

"*You're* not worried?"

"Why should I be?"

"Apparently someone suspects you so strongly that they're paying money to a private detective agency to have you shadowed."

"Of course," said Johnny, "we don't know for sure that *I'm* the one who's being shadowed."

Linda inhaled sharply. "You think — me?"

"Have you been behaving yourself lately?"

Linda looked thoughtfully at Johnny. "You're not really joking. You think I — "

"No."

"You do!"

Johnny sighed lightly. "At this stage of the game, I suspect everybody. You say you weren't at the plant yesterday, but your father owns the place, your brother works there and you've probably been in and out of it a thousand times. You may or may not be aware of people in the factory. Let's say you're not, but there isn't one of those five hundred odd workers, male and female, who doesn't know about you. It's an old company. I know of two employees who have been with the company for thirty-nine years. They know the day you were born; you may never have talked to them, but they know you and everything about you . . ."

"But I don't see how that could involve me in a brutal murder."

"You know about your father being called The Duke?"

She nodded. "Yes. The newspapers have always called him The Leather Duke."

"And the employees, in talking about him, refer to him as The Duke. They speak of you as The Duchess. The Towner Leather Company is an island

157

in the city, an independent principality. The workers are its citizens. Some of them love the rulers, some of them hate them. But *all* fear them . . . "

"Why should they fear us?"

"Everybody fears his employer. Any workman can be fired, lose his security. A word of praise for one of the rulers, or a word of hate, can be resented by another employee. The reason for a quarrel does not determine the degree of hate that is engendered. A blow is struck and . . . " Johnny shrugged.

"You make it sound very devious," Linda said soberly.

"The reasons for murder are usually devious. You take Al Piper; from all I've heard about him he was a pretty decent sort, a married man with two children. A pretty steady worker, as witness his long employment at the Towner factory. He had only one really bad habit; he was a periodic drinker. Twice a year he went on binges . . . "

"But you don't know what he did during those drinking periods? I understand he had just come off one a couple of days ago."

"True, but I want to call attention to the fact that he wasn't killed while he was on one of those binges. It was only after he had sobered up and returned to work. I think therefore that his death can be traced to something that happened at the plant. It points the finger at a Towner man — or woman."

"Of whom there are five hundred."

"My job is to eliminate and keep on eliminating until only one person is left — the murderer."

13

THE man from the Wiggins Detective Agency followed Johnny and Linda Towner back to the leather factory.

"Now," Johnny said, "we'll see whether he's following you or me. I'll go in and you drive off."

"But I wanted to see Dad," protested Linda.

"He won't be back yet from his directors' meeting," said Johnny, "and me, I've got to get to work."

Linda hesitated, then nodded agreement. "All right, I'll see you later."

She stayed in her car and Johnny went into the plant. He stopped inside the door, however, and peered out through the glass. Linda started up the Cadillac convertible and drove off.

The man in the black Chevrolet continued to loll back in his seat. Johnny nodded thoughtfully. "Well, that settles that. He's watching me."

He climbed up to the office floor and was so wrapped in thought that he did not see Nancy Miller. She started to speak to him, then thought better of the idea. Johnny rang for the elevator, then saw Nancy.

He hurried back to her. "Eight o'clock this evening," he said.

"Eight o'clock, what?"

"That's when I'll pick you up. Oh, I haven't got your address."

"Aren't you taking a lot for granted?" Nancy Miller asked, coolly.

"Why no, you said you'd go out with me if I weren't a laborer and I'm no longer toiling with my hands."

"Then why're you going upstairs?"

"I'll tell you about that this evening. Here's the elevator. The address . . . "

She hesitated, then suddenly smiled. "635 Armitage."

"Eight o'clock — your best dress!"

He stepped into the elevator and rode up to the counter floor. He walked through to the sorting department and noted that it was ten minutes after two.

Hal Johnson was leaning against his

161

desk. He looked up at the clock and then at Johnny.

"Hiyah, Hal," Johnny greeted him cheerfully.

Johnson grunted. "Go out to lunch with Mr. Towner?" he asked, sarcastically.

"No, his daughter."

Johnson blinked. "All right," he said, "I'm only the foreman here. Maybe I'm not supposed to know what's going on. I hired you for a counter sorter yesterday, and today the boss calls you down to his office and you have lunch with his daughter."

"The office send up the John B. Croft order yet?"

"What Croft order?"

"The one I got just before lunch. Twenty barrels."

"*You* got an order for counters from the Croft Shoe Company?"

"Yes, Mr. Towner wanted to find out if I was a good salesman." Johnny shrugged. "So I ran over and got the order."

Johnson groaned. "Now, I've heard everything."

Johnny leaned toward the counter

162

foreman. "Harry offered me the sales manager's job."

"Oh, no!" cried Johnson.

"Don't worry, Hal," Johnny said easily, "I turned it down."

Johnson looked at Johnny a moment, then swallowed hard.

"Just a minute," he said, thickly.

He left Johnny at the head of the sorting benches and strode down the line to where Elliott Towner was working at his bench. Johnny saw Johnson ask young Towner a question. He didn't hear Elliott's reply, but saw Johnson stagger as if struck by an invisible fist. Towner, however, continued to talk and Johnson listened intently for a moment or two. Then he bobbed his head and came back toward Johnny.

As the foreman approached Johnny saw that his face was filmed with perspiration. "I'm fifty-two years old," Johnson said when he came up. "I've worked for this company since I was thirteen — thirty-nine years. I've seen a lot of men come and go here, Fletcher. I've hired thousands of men and I've fired a few hundred. But, so help me, I've never had

163

a man here like you . . . " He cleared his throat. "And *I* hired you!"

"You almost didn't," said Johnny. "Sam Cragg was your first choice. By the way, where is Sam?"

"Piling up barrels," said Johnson. "Without Joe Genara — and without the elevator. Now, don't tell me you're going to pull him off that job."

"How could *I* pull him off?" asked Johnny, innocently. "You're the foreman."

"I am?"

"Of course."

"I thought you were taking over!"

"Me? Whatever gave you that idea?"

"Elliott said that you — "

"Shh," said Johnny. "I'm going to snoop around here, that's all. A little undercover work, until I smoke out the man who killed Al Piper. But don't pay any attention to me. I won't interfere with the work."

"Will the work interfere with you?"

Johnny chuckled. "Not if I don't have to do any of it."

About eight pairs of eyes down the line of benches were watching Johnny and the foreman, while the owners were pretending to be sorting counters.

Johnny clapped Johnson on the shoulder and at least six audible gasps went up along the benches. Johnny left the foreman at his high bookkeeper's desk and headed for an aisle between two rows of barrels. He reached the washbasins at the rear, stopped to listen and heard the thump of a barrel on concrete. He headed to the left and saw Sam lifting a barrel of counters over his head.

"Johnny!" Sam cried. "I was just thinkin' that you ran out on me . . . "

He eased the barrel on top of a stack of three, then turned happily to Johnny. "Where'd you get the two bucks you left for me? I sure had a swell lunch and I still got ninety cents."

"I've got about four-ninety, myself," said Johnny. "Four hundred and ninety." He took the bills from his pocket and exhibited them to Sam.

Sam gasped. "Johnny, you didn't rob . . . ?"

"Now, Sam, you know I wouldn't do a thing like that. Mr. Towner gave me the money — an advance."

"You conned him out of it?" Then

165

Sam grimaced. "It'll take us about a year to earn that, Johnny." Sam's voice rose in agony. "You ain't gonna make us work here that long, are you?"

"You can ease off now, Sam. We're back in the chips."

"And we're quittin'?"

"Well, not exactly." Johnny coughed gently. "I sold Mr. Towner on the idea of letting me find the murderer of Al Piper."

"No, Johnny, you didn't!"

"I'm afraid I did."

"But you promised me you wouldn't do any more detective stuff."

"I made no such promise, Sam. As a matter of fact, we were already working on the job. Only we were doing it for nothing. Now, we're doing it for pay."

"But that cop was up here again this morning, Johnny. He was askin' all sorts of questions. About you — and me . . ."

"I know. He tried a little joust with me just before lunch. He came off second-best."

"Maybe, Johnny, maybe. But don't forget they got rooms down at Headquarters

166

where they make you sit under a big white light and ask you a lot of questions with rubber hoses and things. We wouldn't come out so good on that, would we?"

"That isn't going to happen to us Sam. I'm way ahead of Lieutenant Lindstrom right now. While he's making up his mind, I'll grab the murderer."

"Now?"

"Well, no. I don't know who he is."

"You got any idea, yet?"

"Uh-uh. Let's see, it was over in the next aisle you found him. Let's take a look."

"Do we have to?"

"Cut it out, Sam. The man's dead. His body was taken away yesterday morning."

Sam frowned, but followed Johnny reluctantly into the next aisle. "Now, let's go at this scientifically," Johnny said. "There are ten stacks of barrels on each side — "

"Only nine on the right side," Sam said. "The empty place is where, ah, Al Piper was . . . "

"That's right."

Johnny walked into the aisle. "Four

stacks of barrels, then this empty spot, then five stacks — mmm." Johnny stepped past the empty spot in the row of barrels where the body of Piper had been found and continued on to the other end of the aisle.

A rack had been built here, running the entire length of the counter sorting department. Partly filled barrels were piled on the rack and under it, more or less screening the sorting department from the stacks. But by stooping, Johnny could see under the rack and over the top of the barrels set on the floor, into the sorting department.

Johnny put his eye to the shaft. He found himself watching the back of the nearest counter sorter — Elliott Towner. He looked thoughtfully at the back of the Leather Duke's son, for a long moment, then shifted his glance to the next bench. It was vacant, Sam Cragg's place. Beyond it, on the left, Joe Genara was working and to the left of him two men with whom Johnny had not yet got acquainted. Past them was Cliff Goff, the horse player. Then came Johnny's bench and, finally, at the very end, next to

Johnson's desk, the bench of old Axel Swensen.

As Johnny looked, Karl Kessler, the assistant foreman, came walking into the sorting department. He said a word or two to Swensen, then stopped at Johnny's bench and began idly resorting some of the bunches of counters Johnny had piled up early that morning.

Sam moved up behind Johnny and bent down. "What're you looking at, Johnny?" he whispered.

"Men at work," replied Johnny.

"Jeez," Sam exclaimed suddenly. "Maybe the murderer was watchin' us workin' yesterday morning." He shivered. "Gives you a funny feeling."

"What I can't figure out," said Johnny, "is why Al Piper came back here in the first place. He ran a skiving machine, which is out in the main room."

"Maybe he came back here to meet, uh, whoever it was who killed him."

"Which meant that he knew the man."

"Yeah, sure."

"But why couldn't he talk to him out in the open?"

"You asking me, Johnny, or yourself?"

169

"Myself, I guess."

Johnny sighed and rose to his full length. "What time did you come back here to help Joe with the barrels yesterday, Sam?"

"I didn't look at the clock, Johnny, but I guess it was about a half hour after we started to work."

"That would have been around ten o'clock, and it was an hour or so before you found him here. But he'd been dead for an hour to two hours then. In other words, he could have been killed as early as nine o'clock . . . "

"At that time we weren't even working here yet."

"Cut it out, Sam," exclaimed Johnny. "*We* know we didn't kill him."

"That's right," exclaimed Sam. "We know that."

"And one other person knows we didn't do it — the murderer."

Sam looked about uneasily. "You know, Johnny, I don't like working here. I keep thinking somebody's watching me. It's too dark and too many places to hide. A guy could throw a knife at you before you knew it."

Johnny snapped his fingers. "Sam, you've done it!"

"What've I done?"

"Given me my first clue. The knife."

"But the copper said it was *your* knife!"

"*I* know it wasn't my knife, Sam. Think back — when you found Al Piper and we were all nosing around here, there was no sign of any knife. It wasn't until later that Lindstrom found my knife, back here. Planted. Yet Piper was killed with a knife."

"Yeah, sure, but I don't get your point. The guy who done it didn't want to leave his knife laying here, because it could be traced to him."

"Right, Sam — to a certain point. There are a lot of knives around here; every counter sorter has one. But if it was stolen from one of the benches it would be missed in a matter of minutes, because the sorters are always using their knives to trim leather. For the same reason, the sorters — if one of them was the murderer — wouldn't use his own knife to do the job. He couldn't be sure he'd have time enough to really wash the knife

171

thoroughly, without being seen. Those leather knives are eight inches long, sharp as razors and with long points. You can't fold them so you can't carry them around in your pocket." Johnny drew a deep breath. "So it's my idea that the murderer didn't use a leather knife at all. He used a folding pocketknife, which he could put into his pocket without washing. Then he got to worrying about that, was afraid there might be a search and blood found on his clothes, so he stole one of the knives from the bench and dumped it here."

"And he just picked your knife by accident?"

"Maybe," said Johnny. "And maybe not. I was a new man on the job. The police would waste a lot of time trying to ferret out the history of a man nobody around here knew anything about."

"The cops couldn't find out much about us, the way we've always moved around," Sam said. "Of course, if they took our fingerprints . . . "

"Speaking of fingerprints, I wonder if Lieutenant Lindstrom went over that knife of mine that was planted here.

172

I guess I'll never know the answer to that because Lindstrom isn't in much of a co-operating mood. Anything we learn we've got to dig up ourselves. And I guess we might as well get started."

"How?"

"Go back to your bench and talk — talk to everyone you can. If they get sore, fine; people spill things when they're mad. Talk about the murder."

"What about work?"

"Keep on working. At least enough to make it look good."

14

THEY started out of the aisle, went to the one that cut through to the counter sorting department. As they came through, they ran into Karl Kessler, about to go into the aisle.

"Hey," exclaimed Kessler, "you two guys are the biggest stallers in the place." He nodded to Sam. "You finish piling up the barrels?"

"Unh-uh," replied Sam.

"Then get busy."

"Sam's going to sort counters a while," said Johnny easily. "He's tired lifting up barrels."

"Tired or not, the barrels got to get piled up. Get back on the job. You can use the elevator; Joe'll help you."

"Do I have to?" Sam asked uneasily, looking at Johnny.

"No," Johnny said. "Go and sort counters."

Kessler exclaimed: "Somebody make you boss around here, Fletcher?"

174

"Why don't you ask Johnson?"

"I guess maybe I will. I heard you were down in Harry Towner's office all morning."

"Not all morning, Karl."

Kessler regarded him suspiciously, then without another word, turned on his heel and went off, apparently to find Hal Johnson.

Johnny nodded to Sam and the latter went to his bench. Johnny strolled back to his own bench. He looked at old Axel Swensen. The former sailor was working furiously, an intent scowl on his face. On the right of Johnny, Cliff Goff was picking up counters leisurely, feeling them and putting them into bunches. His head was bent to his work, but his eyes were almost glazed.

His mind was miles away, probably at Belmont or Arlington Park, booting home a winner.

Johnny said quietly: "What's good today?"

"Honeymoon'll win the sixth in a gallop," replied Cliff Goff. Then he blinked and looked at Johnny. "New man?" he asked.

175

"Pretty new," said Johnny. "I started yesterday morning."

"Yeah, guess you did. Your face is familiar."

"Kinda new here yourself, aren't you?"

"Me? I been here nine years. I guess it's nine years. Maybe ten."

"You have a hard time remembering such minor details," Johnny observed.

"I get a *Racing Form* in the morning on my way to work," said Cliff Goff. "It takes me seventeen minutes to ride down on the streetcar. In that time I got to memorize the weight, the post position and the jockey for every horse running at two, sometimes three tracks."

"That takes a pretty good memory," Johnny suggested.

Goff nodded acknowledgment. "You ain't kidding. Then while I'm sorting counters I got to figure out the chances of every horse and I got to put down my bets on the eastern horses by twelve o'clock and the western by one."

"That takes care of you until one o'clock. What do you think about in the afternoon?"

"Yesterday's races. How the horses ran

176

and why. Takes time and concentration."

"You mean with all that thinking you give it, you don't win every race?"

"Horses are honest, but owners aren't. A horse gallops six furlongs in 1:11 on a fast track. That's pretty good time, but an owner puts a horse like that in a race and he goes to the post at even money. So he runs him for the exercise, comes in sixth — in 1:13. Next week he runs him and the odds are two to one. The horse comes in eighth. He loses three-four more races and he's twelve to one. Well, that's a decent price and the owner might run the horse the next time; on the other hand, he may be waiting for a real killing and hold the horse until he's forty to one. You see, I've got to put myself in the place of the owner, and figure out what I'd do if I was in his place."

"I know what I'd do," said Johnny. "I'd give up horses and take up crossword puzzles."

"I can't quit," said Goff. "I'm too far behind."

Johnny shook his head and turning, moved over nearer to Axel Swensen.

"Well, Cap'n Swensen," he said

cheerfully, "how's it today?"

"I like my yob," Swensen said, without looking at Johnny. "I need the money."

"Don't we all?"

"You don't make me say things I don't want to say," Swensen went on fiercely. "I mind my own business, work hard, don't bother anybody."

"I'm sure of that," said Johnny, "but you've got eyes to see and ears to hear, whether you're bothering anyone else or not. Somebody stole the knife from this bench yesterday."

"No," said Swensen desperately, "I don't see anybody taking knife. I am an old man. I cannot find new yob."

"All right," said Johnny, "we'll let it ride."

He drummed on the bench with his fingers, then whirled and headed for the far end of the sorting benches where Sam Cragg was engaged in a heated conversation with Elliott Towner. As he came up, Sam was saying:

"You can squawk all you want, but it's Johnny who'll get him in the end, you wait and see."

"Thanks, Sam," said Johnny. Then to

178

Elliott: "Sam's right. I'll get him."

"And what'll you do when you get him?" asked Elliott sarcastically. "Talk him to death?"

Johnny chuckled. "You know, Elliott, I've got a strange idea that you don't like me."

"Well, since you brought it up, Fletcher — I don't. I think you're a four-flushing windbag. You've sold my father a bill of goods, but that's always been Dad's one weakness: he's a sucker for peculiar characters."

"He's done pretty well, for a man with a weakness. By the way, how are *you* doing?"

"I'm doing all right," snapped Elliott.

"I'm glad to hear that. How about fixing us up with a guest card at the Lakeside Athletic?"

Elliott Towner stared at Johnny, wide-eyed. "Have you gone completely crazy?"

"No," said Johnny. "I like the Lakeside Club. There's nothing like a good steam and rubdown after a hard day's work, then a good soft bed afterwards. We had to sleep in a flophouse on Halsted Street last night . . . "

"You got some money from Dad, you can go to a hotel."

"I'd rather stay at the Lakeside — at least until I've cleaned up this business."

Elliott hesitated. "If I refuse to get the guest cards for you, you'll go to Dad?"

"Yes."

"There'll be cards waiting for you at the club tonight."

"Thanks, Elliott, that's nice cooperating. Now, do you suppose you could crowd it a little more?"

"You've crowded me too far already."

"This is business. Did you know Al Piper?"

"I didn't start to work here until Monday. Al didn't show up for work until yesterday morning . . . "

"At eight o'clock. He wasn't killed until nine."

Elliott shook his head. "Piper wasn't even a name to me until after he was dead. I never heard of him before, I never saw him."

"But he was killed right behind you, not more than thirty feet away. Uh, you didn't hear anything?"

"I heard nothing. With those machines

180

out in the other room, you can't hear yourself think most of the time. Then they were piling up barrels back here . . . "

"I didn't start piling 'em up until ten o'clock," Sam cut in. "Hey!" He suddenly whirled and headed for Joe Genara. "Hey, Joe, you were piling up barrels yesterday when I came to help you . . . "

Joe Genara grinned, showing even white teeth. "I was gettin' the barrels ready for piling, big boy. I'm not as strong as you are. I gotta use the elevator and with it, it takes two men to pile up the barrels. One to put them on the elevator and ride up with the barrel and the other to crank the thing. That's what Carmella was doing when he got sore and quit."

Johnny moved up quickly beside Sam. "Carmella was helping you back there, yesterday morning?"

"Sure, him and me usually did the piling when there was piling to do."

"You started at eight o'clock yesterday morning?"

"Five-ten minutes after eight."

"And he worked with you until he got fired?"

181

"Who says he got fired?"

"Didn't he?"

"Nah, he quit. Kessler came back and started jawing at him and Carmella got sore and walked off the job."

"What was Kessler complaining about?"

"Well, Carmella wasn't the fastest worker in the world."

"'Small pay, small work,'" quoted Sam.

"Sure, he was always saying that."

"You said it to me yesterday."

"I got it from Carmella. He never hurt himself working. Count twelve-thirteen hundred pairs of counters a day. Take all morning to pile up a dozen barrels."

"With you helping him," suggested Johnny.

Joe shrugged. "Takes two people to pile up barrels. I still had to wait for him to do the cranking."

Johnny nodded. "While you were piling up barrels yesterday, or with Carmella, did Al Piper happen to come along?"

"No," said Joe quickly.

"What time did Carmella quit the job?"

"We'd only been working about a half

hour or so when Kessler came up and started squawking. They went at it for a few minutes, then Carmella said the hell with it . . . about quarter to nine, I'd say."

"You stayed back with the barrels, after Carmella walked off the job?"

"No, I came back here, for ten-fifteen minutes. Then Kessler told me to go back and get the barrels ready and he'd have someone else help me in a little while." Joe nodded to Sam. "I was only back there a little while when you came along."

"I think," said Johnny slowly, "that you've set the time of the murder pretty accurately — between a quarter to nine when Carmella got sore and quit his job, and nine o'clock when you came back here to get more barrels ready for further stacking."

"Could be," said Joe Genara.

Johnny caught Sam's eye and walked off a few feet. "Sam, I've got to run out for an hour or two. Maybe longer. You stick around here and keep on talking to people."

"You'll be back by five?"

"I hope so, but if I should happen to get tied up, go down to the Lakeside Athletic Club. Elliott's fixing us up with guest cards. Get a good double room and wait for me."

"All right, Johnny, but try to get back here by five o'clock, will you?"

"I will."

Johnny started down the aisle, past Johnson's desk, then whirled back and scooped up the telephone directory. He found a number, nodded and left.

Down in the office Nancy Miller looked at Johnny in surprise.

"Knocking off for the day?"

"Nope, Taffy, believe it or not, I'm working. In case I don't get back before five, remember eight o'clock."

He winked at her and left the building.

15

ACROSS the street the Wiggins man in the black Chevrolet came to attention. Johnny waved at him, then pointed in the direction of Larrabee Street.

As he reached the corner of Larrabee Street he looked over his shoulder. The Chevrolet was crawling to a halt at the curb a short distance away.

Johnny looked down Larrabee Street and saw a taxicab approaching. He stepped into the street, held up his hand and the cab screeched to a halt. Johnny got in.

"Randolph and Wells," he said.

The cab jerked off, scooted to Chicago Avenue and turned east. At Wells it turned right and a moment later, the cab driver spoke to Johnny.

"Its none a my business, Mister, but I think there's a car following us. Black Chevvie."

"Yes," said Johnny. "Fella breaking in

a set of tires for me."

The driver thought that over for a moment, then tried again. "We ain't got far to go, but I can lose him."

"Don't bother."

The driver shrugged and pulled up at the corner of Randolph and Wells, a few minutes later. Johnny got out and giving the man a dollar looked back. The black Chevrolet was pulling in to the curb.

Johnny grinned and crossing Randolph started looking at the building numbers. Halfway down the block he turned into a rickety old building, consulted the directory, then rode in the elevator to the fourth floor.

He stepped out in front of a ground glass door on which was lettered: *Wiggins Detective Agency. Enter.*

Johnny entered.

A grey-haired woman with horn-rim spectacles sat at a battered desk in a tiny reception room. One office door opened off the room.

"Mr. Wiggins," Johnny said.

"You have an appointment?"

"No, but I — well, I'm looking for a good detective agency and you were

186

highly recommended . . . "

"By whom?"

Johnny shook his head. "He asked me not to tell. Of course if Mr. Wiggins can't see me . . . "

"What's the nature of your trouble?"

"I'm not in trouble, but let it pass; there's another agency in the next block and — "

"Just a moment!"

The woman got up, opened the private office door and went in. She closed the door behind her. Johnny leaned across the desk, saw a pad of paper on which there was some writing. He swung the pad around, whistled softly. The writing read: "Begley phoned. Said subject went into leather factory. Girl drove off. Begley is waiting outside factory."

He had just flipped the pad of paper back into its former position and straightened when the inner door opened and the receptionist came out. Her eyes went from Johnny, near the desk, to the pad of paper.

"Mr. Wiggins will see you," she said, severely.

Johnny went into the private office.

An enormously fat, bald man swung a squeaking swivel chair around, but did not get up.

"I'm Ed Wiggins," he wheezed. "Have a seat."

Johnny sat down on a cracked straight-backed chair.

"Perhaps I made a mistake," he began, "I was under the impression that this was a, well, *large* private detective agency."

"Ain't I big enough?" snapped Wiggins.

"Plenty," Johnny retorted, "but the job I have in mind requires the services of a couple of operators and you apparently run this place alone . . ."

"I do the brain work," said Wiggins, angrily, "I've got the best crew of operators working for me that you could find in the whole city . . ."

"They make their headquarters in the phone booth down in the lobby?"

Wiggins banged a fat fist on his desk, almost splintering it. "You come in here to make cracks or hire a detective? My men work on a fee basis. When I need them they go to work; when I haven't got anything for them, they stay home. How many men do you need?"

188

"Three."

"I got the three best men in town, Joe Carmichael, Jim White and Les Begley. Shadowing, Begley's your man, bodyguard, Carmichael, and White's the lad for schmoosing up to the ladies. What's your problem?"

"A little of all three," said Johnny. "I want to find out everything there is to know about a man — his family life, his friends, his enemies, the things he did, the places he went. Everything there is to know."

"Cost you money."

"I didn't expect you to do it for fun."

Wiggins leaned over his desk with somewhat of an effort and picked up a pencil. "What'd you say your name was?"

"I didn't."

Wiggins grunted. "Smith, huh? All right. Now, what's the name of the party you want investigated?"

"Piper. Al Piper."

Wiggins started to write, but hadn't scrawled more than the initial letter when he stopped and looked up at Johnny.

"What's the gag? Piper's dead."

"How do you know?"

"I can read the newspapers, can't I? He was murdered yesterday, in a leather factory up on the north side."

The phone on Wiggins' desk tinkled. He scooped it up. "Yeah? What . . . ? All right, put him on . . . Hello. Yes . . . what's that? I see . . . all right. Stay on the job." He hung up, leaned back in his swivel chair and folded his fat hands across the wide expanse of his stomach.

"Smith, huh? Spell it F-l-e-t-c-h-e-r, huh?"

"Improved spelling," said Johnny. He nodded to the phone. "Begley? The one who's good at shadowing?"

"What's the game?"

"No game, Wiggins. I want to hire a good detective agency . . . "

"You can't hire this one. It's against the rules to take two clients on the one job . . . " He hesitated. "That is if their interests, are, ah, inimical?"

"Well, are they?"

"Look, Fletcher, I know damn well that your being here isn't any coincidence.

190

You found out this noon that Begley was shadowing you and that he worked for me. That's why you came here, isn't it?"

Johnny looked coolly at the detective, then drew his money from his pocket. He extracted a hundred dollar bill, put the rest of the money back, then smoothed out the hundred dollar bill and held it up. During the entire process Wiggins' eyes remained glued on the bill.

"Exhibit A," said Johnny, "a hale and hearty hundred dollar bill."

"Very pretty."

"Isn't it? Now, what can I buy with it?"

"You can buy one good private detective for four days, or two men for two days."

"What else will it buy?"

Wiggins continued to stare at the bill and began to wheeze. "Nothing."

"You're sure of that, Wiggins? Because in just thirty seconds I'm going to put this back into my pocket and it'll stay there."

"What do you want?" Wiggins cried.

"One word. Just one little word. The

name of the person who hired you to shadow me."

"I — I can't tell you that," groaned Wiggins. Then he reached forward, grabbed up a pencil and scrawled on a slip of paper. "I can't tell you, but . . . " He deliberately swung his swivel chair around, so that his back was to Johnny.

Johnny leaned forward and glanced at the piece of paper on which was written a single word: *Wendland*.

"I'll be damned!" exclaimed Johnny. "I didn't think he had it in him." He dropped the hundred dollar bill on the desk.

Wiggins swiveled back, passed a fat hand over his desk and the hundred dollar bill disappeared. Johnny looked at him thoughtfully, then went through the business of taking another hundred dollar bill from his pocket.

"Now, to the business we started to discuss before — Al Piper . . . "

"You still want that?"

"Yes. Send a man down to Piper's neighborhood. Have him talk to Mrs. Piper, the neighbors. Find out everything there is to know about his personal life, how he got along with his wife, the neighbors. Have a second man work the neighborhood taverns, the grocers, any place he might have traded. I don't want to know how many bottles of whiskey he bought — I'm interested in the people he might have talked to in places like that; strangers he picked arguments with, while drunk. Especially the past twelve days."

"We can do that, all right," said Wiggins. He looked at the hundred dollar bill in Johnny's hands. "Two men, for two days?"

"No, they can get all that in one day — two men, for one day each. A third man to check up on one Carmella Vitali, who lives in the vicinity of Oak and Milton."

"Check. He's a prime suspect. Who else?"

Johnny thought a moment, then screwing up his face, said: "Harry Towner."

"The leather man?"

"The Duke, himself."

"It's none of my business how you spend your money," said Wiggins, "but

I've been reading up on this case. I hardly think it likely that a man like Towner would have anything in common with this Piper fellow."

"Piper worked for Towner," Johnny said, "and so did everyone connected with this case."

Wiggins frowned. "What do you want us to find out about Towner? It isn't easy to check up on a man like that."

"I know, but on the other hand, he's practically a public figure. The newspapers undoubtedly have a great deal of information on him in their files. I'm not a Chicagoan; things you people know about him, I don't. I'd like to get a sketch of his career — business, as well as personal."

"Well, that we can do."

"Good, get your men busy. Let's see, it's four o'clock now; I'm paying you for four good men until four o'clock tomorrow afternoon. We'll see then about continuing."

"You want reports before tomorrow?"

"Yes. I'll call in. You have night telephone service, I suppose?"

"Oh yes. Granite 3–1127. My operators

are supposed to report every hour if they can. But where can we reach you if something important develops?"

"The Lakeside Athletic Club. Leave a message if I'm not there."

Johnny handed Wiggins the other hundred dollar bill and prepared to leave. "You're sure now that this isn't inimical to Fred Wendland's interests?"

"Wendland?" asked Wiggins. "Who's Wendland?"

"All right," said Johnny, "you haven't said a word to me."

Wiggins smiled weakly and Johnny left the office. Down on the street, he walked to the black Chevrolet. Begley, the Wiggins operator, regarded him sourly. "Things have changed, Begley. Better call Wiggins for new instructions."

Begley shrugged, but made no reply.

"I'm going to the Lakeside Athletic Club," said Johnny. "I'll be inside for quite awhile so you'll have time to telephone. On second thought, why don't you give me a lift over to Michigan Avenue?"

"Beat it," snarled Begley.

"Unsociable guy," said Johnny and walked off.

He went to Madison and turned east. A few minutes later, he entered the Athletic Club. "Fletcher's the name," he said, to the doorman. "My friend, Elliott Towner, said he was leaving a guest card here for me . . ."

"Oh yes, the office phoned a few minutes ago. For Mr. Fletcher and Mr. Cragg, all the privileges of the club."

"That's right, Mr. Cragg will arrive about five-thirty. You can send him right up."

"Thank you, sir."

Johnny entered the lobby of the club and saw a regular hotel desk, on the right. He stepped up to it.

"Mr. Elliott Towner's arranged for a guest card for me," he said, to the clerk. "John Fletcher."

"Very happy to have you with us, Mr. Fletcher. You'd like a room?"

"A double room, with twin beds. Mr. Cragg will be joining me shortly."

"Very good, sir. Mr. Towner also arranged for Mr. Cragg. I have a very lovely suite overlooking the boulevard.

Two rooms, with connecting bath. Do you wish us to send anywhere for your luggage?"

"Why, no," said Johnny. "I've already arranged for it to be sent over."

"Very good, sir. I'll have a boy show you up. Front!"

197

16

A UNIFORMED bellboy came quickly across the lobby. The clerk slid a key over the counter. "Show Mr. Fletcher to 612."

"This way, sir," said the bellboy.

Johnny followed him to the elevators and up to the sixth floor. There the boy led him to the front of the building and unlocked the door of Room 612.

"One of the best suites in the Club," the bellboy said. He led Johnny through the bathroom into the adjoining room, flicking on lights along the way.

Passing through the bathroom, Johnny saw a placard on the back of the door. It was headed: 'Club Rules.'

Rule #1 in bold-face type was: NO TIPPING OF EMPLOYEES.

"What's this?" exclaimed Johnny, tapping the sign. "No tipping?"

"Just one of the rules, sir."

"That's too bad."

"Oh, hardly anyone pays any attention

to it," the bellboy said brightly.

"But I'm only a guest of the club, not a member. I wouldn't want to violate the rules and get Elliott Towner in bad."

"Towner?" said the bellboy. "If that was the only thing he had to worry about . . . "

"Quite a lad, isn't he?"

The bellboy shrugged and tried to pass Johnny in the bathroom. But Johnny pulled out his dwindling roll of bills, and began looking through them.

"Tell me about Elliott," he said, carelessly. "Been cutting up around here, has he?"

"I wouldn't know, sir. I'm only a bellboy."

"Bellboys know everything that goes on. You started to say something about Elliott a moment ago . . . "

"I'm sorry, sir, I should have kept my mouth shut."

Johnny shuffled the bills in his hands. "You've got me curious, so you might as well spill it. What's Towner got to worry about?"

The bellboy looked steadily at the money in Johnny's hands. Johnny extracted a five dollar bill, creased it lengthwise and handed it to the boy.

"You were going to say . . . ?"

"Dames!" blurted the bellboy. "They ain't allowed in the club, exceptin' in the dinin' rooms, so I'm on the split shift last night and this dame comes bustin' into the lobby and says she's gotta see him. Gus, the doorman, knocks off at eleven, so he ain't on the door and she's in the lobby and headin' for the elevator before I can head her off. She gives me quite a workout, too. Course, I don't mind that, cause she's a looker and if a looker wants to rassle a fall or two with me, it's okay, but then Homer the bell captain, comes up from the steam room where he's sneakin' one and I get holy hell for lettin' her in. On'y I didn't."

"She said she wanted to see Elliott Towner?"

"No-no, I get that from Nora."

"Nora?"

"The telephone operator. Nora and me are, well, we go out some a the nights I'm working the dog watch. That's the way we work here, one day from twelve noon to eight in the evening, then the next day, seven to twelve in the morning, off in the afternoon, then six to midnight."

"Congratulations," said Johnny, drily. "I hope you and Nora will be very happy . . . "

"Huh? We ain't talkin' about gettin' married, nothin' like that."

"All right, then do you mind telling me what you got from Nora?"

"The stuff about this dame and Towner. She calls up all evenin', eight-ten calls and she don't get him. She leaves messages and Towner don't call back."

"He was here?"

"That's what I'm telling you, ain't I? He's here, but he tells Nora he's out, so the dame keeps callin' and leavin' messages. Important, she says, matter of life and death. So Nora feels sorry for her and just before she's going off duty, when the call comes in . . . "

The bellboy stopped, scowling.

"Go on," cried Johnny.

"No, I've talked too much already. As long as it was only me in it . . . "

Johnny whisked off a ten dollar bill and thrust it into the bellboy's hand. "Keep talking."

201

The boy ran the tip of his tongue around his lips, drew a deep breath. "She put the call through to Towner's room."

"And?"

"That's all."

"For ten dollars?" Johnny snarled. "Give me back that dough." He lunged for the ten dollar bill which was still in the bellboy's hand. But the latter drew back.

"All right, Nora listened in. Towner was sore as a bear with a boil on his tail, when he found out who it was, but he shut up when this girl let him have it. Of course, Nora didn't know what she was talking about, but whatever it was, it cooled off Mr. Towner."

"What was it she said?"

"I dunno. Nora couldn't figure it out. Said it wasn't so much *what* she said — "

"What was it she said?"

"Only something about: 'I know who did it,' but it certainly had an effect on Towner. He shut up right away and when he said he'd see her today, he was as meek as a mouse . . . This was after we threw her out here, about eleven-thirty you know. Around midnight — "

202

"This girl, did she give her name?"

"On the telephone? Unh-uh. On'y when she left the messages before. Just — 'Nancy called' . . . "

"Nancy!" cried Johnny.

"Yeah, Nancy?" The bellboy's eyes slitted. "Know her?"

"No," said Johnny.

"I been thinkin' today," the bellboy went on, "Towner's old man owns a big leather factory up on the north side and there was a murder there yesterday and I was thinkin' — "

"Don't," said Johnny, "don't think."

"Yeah, maybe you're right. Uh, what I been tellin' you, that's just between us, huh? You could cost me my job, maybe. And Nora — "

"Don't worry. Not a word to anyone."

"Thanks, and, uh, if you need anything, just call the bell stand and ask for Number Three. If you forget the number, ask for Augie . . . "

"Augie, Number Three; I'll remember."

Augie, Number 3, stowed away his haul of fifteen dollars and left the suite.

Johnny made a quick tour through the suite, then stepped to a desk and found

203

some club stationery. He picked up a pen and wrote: "Sam, come down to the steam room."

He stuck the message in the frame of the dresser mirror where it would be seen readily and, leaving the suite, rode down in the elevator to the steam room. An attendant showed him to a locker room and gave him a towel and a sheet. Draping the sheet around him he stepped into the hot air room.

There were several wooden deck chairs scattered about the room, two or three of which were occupied by nude club members. Johnny spread the sheet out over a vacant chair and seated himself on it. Even through the sheet, the wood of the chair was near the scorching point, for the temperature in the room was 180 degrees.

Perspiration broke out on his body inside of a minute or two and in ten minutes it streamed off his body. He remained in the room another ten minutes, then came out and took a hot shower. He finished off with cold water, then ran to the swimming pool and dove in.

He went down deep, came up and looked into the face of Fred Wendland, less then two feet from his own.

"Freddie!" Johnny exclaimed. "Imagine meeting you here."

Treading water, Wendland looked at him blankly a moment, before recognition dawned on him. "Fletcher," he said, then: "How the devil did you get in here?"

"Guest card. And you?"

"I'm a member of this club."

Johnny wasn't good at treading water, so he swam to the edge of the pool. He climbed up and sat down on the tile, dangling his legs in the water. A few feet away, Wendland continued to tread water. His face wore an angry scowl.

"Too bad you ran out this noon," Johnny said, cheerfully. "If you'd hung around I'd've introduced you to the shamus. We had quite a little tête-à-tête."

"I'm not interested in private detectives," snapped Wendland. He swam closer to the edge of the pool, then began treading water again. "And I don't understand why a man like you would want a guest card at this club. As much gall as you've got, you

205

must know that you don't fit in here."

"Why, I thought I was fitting in very well," Johnny replied, mockingly. "I've done a good day's work, so now I'm relaxing at the club. A steam, a little swim, then a rubdown and I'm all set for the evening."

"You know damn well what I meant, Fletcher. The people here aren't your sort."

"They've got two heads and I've only got one?"

"You're a common laborer."

"A common laborer built this swimming pool, Wendland. Common laborers raise the food you eat and make the clothes you wear. And as for me, specifically, Freddie boy . . . " Johnny got to his feet, roused. "Name one thing in which you think you're superior to me. Physically, I can lick the hell out of you . . . "

"That remains to be seen," snarled Wendland.

"And mentally, Freddie, in what respect do you figure you've got it over me? I can make a fool out of you on any subject you name . . . "

"I've had enough from you, Fletcher,"

sputtered Wendland. "Wait until I climb out of here . . . " He swam quickly for the edge of the pool, began to clamber out.

Johnny watched him coolly. "You've admitted it yourself, hiring the Wiggins Detective Agency to shadow me . . . "

Wendland, half out of water, stared at Johnny in astonishment. "Wh-what are you talking about?"

"A man named Begley's been following me all day. He's outside the club right now. He works for the Wiggins Agency. And *you* hired them."

Wendland finished climbing out of the pool, but was no longer belligerent. A confused frown twisted his features.

"Why are you having me shadowed, Wendland?" Johnny continued. "You know damn well I didn't kill Al Piper. So why . . . ? Are you afraid of something I might find out about you?"

Wendland suddenly whirled and walked away from Johnny. Johnny was still looking after him, when Sam Cragg appeared on the far side of the pool. He spied Johnny and waved.

Johnny gestured him to come around

the pool and rose to meet him. "Get yourself a quick steam and a swim, Sam, while I have a rubdown," he said, "then we'll put on the feed bag."

"One of those nice steaks that they cook so badly here, Johnny?" Sam asked.

Johnny chuckled. "We'll force ourselves to eat them." An attendant approached and Sam went off to the locker rooms. Johnny found an idle masseur and went into a cubicle with him, where he stretched out on a rubbing table.

The masseur covered him with a sheet, then peeling it back off one leg, rubbed olive oil on the limb. He gripped it in both hands and began to work on it. He had tremendously powerful fingers and seemed to find every tender muscle. While he worked, he talked.

"New member, sir, aren't you?" he asked.

"Only a guest. Towner put me up."

"Oh, Mr. Towner, the leather man. I give him a rubdown two-three times a week. Wonderful condition for a man his age. Keeps in good shape . . . Mmm, you got a kink in a muscle here." He worked on it and Johnny had to gasp to

208

keep from wincing in pain. The masseur chuckled. "You ought to watch yourself. Don't exercise, don't work."

"Yeah," said Johnny, "you may be right. By the way, just to test your powers of observation — what business would you say I was in?"

The masseur put down the leg, covered it and exposed the other one. "Stocks, Board of Trade. Maybe radio or advertising."

"You wouldn't take me for a laborer?"

"Ha! You? You wouldn't be living at the club, if you was a laborer. Besides you don't have the muscle for it."

"I could be a laborer out of work."

"No sir, you couldn't. I know a gentleman when I see one."

"You think I'm a gentleman?"

"Oh, sure. That's one thing I know — gentlemen. I have worked at this club for nine years. I massage forty-fifty gentlemen a week. Never make a mistake about a gentleman."

"Ever massage Freddie Wendland?"

"Two-three times a month."

"And he's no different than I am?"

"How you mean? He is younger man

than you, but otherwise the same as you — a gentleman."

Johnny grinned and wondered what Wendland would say to that. He relaxed under the probing hands of the masseur and a half hour later got up from the table, feeling five years younger.

Sam was still in the pool, enjoying himself, but he climbed out and both dressed and adjourned to the grill room. They ordered steaks and when they finished eating it was after seven.

Johnny signed the check with a flourish and they left the grill room.

"And now for our date," Johnny said then.

"We got a date?"

"I have," said Johnny.

"With a girl?"

"With what would I have a date? It's the girl with the taffy-colored hair at the plant. Nancy Miller."

Sam brightened. "Say, she's all right. I passed a few words with her myself, this noon." He cleared his throat. "I wonder if she's got a friend."

"Every girl's got a friend, Sam."

"C'n you call her and ask?"

"Mm, that might not be such a good idea. On the phone a girl can make excuses. We'll surprise her and then she'll have to come through with the friend."

"Didn't we do that in St. Louis once? The girl weighed two hundred pounds."

"Yes, but she was affectionate, wasn't she?"

"You ain't kiddin', Johnny, every pound of her was affectionate. I'm gonna hold out for a girl about Nancy's size."

They left the club and had the doorman get a cab for them. Climbing in, Johnny gave the driver Nancy Miller's Armitage Avenue address.

The cabby made an illegal U turn and headed north up Michigan. Behind them a black Chevvie executed the same illegal U turn. Johnny saw the Chevvie in the rear vision mirror and swore. "You can't trust anybody these days."

Sam did not hear him. He was wrapped in heavy thought, pondering about his blind date.

211

17

THE cab rolled up Michigan, got onto Lake Shore Drive and a few minutes later seemed to be lost in the winding drives of Lincoln Park, but the driver executed a series of complicated turns and suddenly swung into Armitage. A few minutes later he pulled up in front of a dingy three-story apartment house.

He got out and opened the door for Johnny and Sam. "Fella been followin' us ever since we left the club," he said.

"Nothing serious," said Johnny. "Just a private eye."

The cabby looked at the apartment house. "Wife trying to get evidence, eh?"

"Wait'll you see the evidence I've got." Johnny took a ten-dollar bill from his pocket. "This is your big night. We're going to make the rounds of some hot spots."

"Swell," said the driver. "I know a couple of dillies if you run out of places."

Johnny and Sam entered the foyer of the apartment house and found the mailboxes. A card under one read: *Miller-Ballard*, 3C.

They climbed the stairs to the third floor and found Apartment 3C. Johnny leaned against the door buzzer and the door was opened in a matter of three seconds by a girl with natural auburn hair and the smoothest complexion Johnny had seen in four years. The girl was fairly tall and weighed about eighty pounds less than the two hundred mark that Sam had complained about. Johnny shot a quick look at Sam, saw that his mouth was gaping.

"Miss Ballard," said Johnny. "May I introduce your date, my friend, Sam Cragg?"

"Right name," said the girl, "wrong date."

"I'm Johnny Fletcher. Let's talk it over . . . "

Nancy Miller appeared behind the redheaded girl. "Johnny!" she cried. She was wearing a long evening dress that must have cost her four or five weekly paychecks.

213

"Your date," said Miss Ballard. "Excuse me." She backed into the apartment and Johnny and Sam followed. Sam's eyes never once left the redheaded girl.

Nancy Miller looked at Sam Cragg, then at Johnny. Her head tilted to one side. Johnny grinned.

"You did say you had a girl friend for Sam, didn't you?"

"No," said Nancy, coolly. "I didn't."

"You mean I forgot to tell you that Sam and I always double-date girls?"

"You didn't mention it. And if you had, I'd have told you that I never double-date . . . ."

Johnny nodded toward Nancy's roommate. "I don't think Sam would mind."

Miss Ballard heard that. "Sorry, chum. I've got a date."

"With your regular boy friend?"

"Yes."

Johnny made a deprecating gesture. "What's one date more or less with a steady? Sam's new, he's different. And he's the strongest man in the world."

"Oh, the strong man Nancy was telling about."

"She's told you about him? And me?"

214

"About you, plenty!"

"Shut up, Jane!" snapped Nancy Miller.

"Go ahead, Janie," urged Johnny. "I like to hear nice things about me."

"Johnny," said Nancy. "I let you make this date against my better judgment. I've got a very dull novel here, from the rental library, but I think I'd just as soon read it as go out with you."

"Now," said Johnny, appeasingly. "I've got a cab waiting downstairs. I'm all set to show you a few very warm spots . . . "

"Like the Bucket of Blood, perhaps?"

"They've got a dance tonight."

"They have one every Friday night." Nancy went to a closet and got out a coat. "What about him?" she asked, nodding to Sam.

"Gordon's been feeling his oats a little too much lately," Jane Ballard suddenly said. "I think I'll stand him up tonight. Do him good!"

"Atta girl!" cried Johnny.

"Oh, boy!" chortled Sam.

"Jane," said Nancy Miller, "if you don't mind . . . "

"Oh, I don't mind," exclaimed Jane

Ballard. "I'll come along for the laughs."

There was a glint in Nancy's blue eyes, but she turned away and got her purse. When she came back the glint was gone. "All right, Fletcher and Cragg, bring on your laughs."

"The first one's waiting downstairs," said Johnny, "a private detective in a black Chevrolet. He's been shadowing me all day . . . "

"If you think I'm going out with a detective following us, you're crazy," Nancy flared.

"What's the difference?" asked Johnny. "I *want* him to follow me. Saves me the trouble of following him."

Nancy stared at Johnny a moment, then she exhaled softly. "Where do you come in on all this, Johnny?"

"I'm an innocent bystander, that's all."

"Innocent bystanders sometimes get hurt."

"Who's going to hurt me? Freddie Wendland? Or — Elliott Towner?"

Nancy whirled away, walked to a wall mirror and put new lips on her mouth, with her lipstick. Jane Ballard, in the meantime, got her purse and coat.

Nancy put away her lipstick. "All right, let's go."

They left the apartment and crossed the sidewalk to the waiting taxicab. Johnny didn't even bother to look for Begley, the private detective. He was parked nearby, no question of that. They all climbed into the cab.

"Somebody's got to sit on somebody's lap," Johnny said, plumping down and pulling Nancy onto his lap. She was stiff and resistant for a moment, but then leaned back against him. Sam shot a disappointed look at Johnny as he took the seat on the far side. Jane seated herself between Johnny and Sam.

The cabby swiveled his head. "Where to?"

"The Bucket of Blood," said Johnny.

"What's that?"

Nancy exclaimed. "Another of your jokes."

"Uh-uh, the name intrigues me. I'd like to see the place."

"I've got on my new dress," Nancy said, angrily. "I thought we were going — "

"Maybe later on. Let's take a look at the Bucket of Blood, first."

"Mister," said the cabby, patiently. "I know a Bucket of Blood down on Wentworth, near 22nd. There's another out on Kedzie Boulevard . . ."

"The one we want is on Clybourn Avenue. The Clybourn Hall, it's called."

"Oh, *that* place!"

The driver meshed gears and the cab shot away. It roared up Armitage to Halsted, turned left and a few minutes later, diagonaled into Clybourn. The brakes squealed and the car came to a stop.

The group got out of the taxi. The building before which they had stopped was an ancient three-story brick affair. The first floor housed a tavern. A wide door and a stairway led up to the second floor. A banner over the doorway announced: *Clybourn Turnverein Dance. $1.00 Admission. Ladies Free.*

"Ladies, free," Johnny exclaimed. "That's sure a break."

"Ladies don't come here," snapped Nancy.

"Nancy, darling," said Jane Ballard sweetly. "Your claws are showing."

"Thank you, dear, for telling me,"

retorted Nancy. "When we get home tonight, I'll file them down."

"Mustn't fight, girls," chided Johnny. "We came here for fun." He caught Nancy's elbow and started up the long flight of stairs.

Music pelted them as they climbed. It wasn't good, but it was loud and that was what the patrons of the Clybourn Hall seemed to want. Although it was still early, there were already three or four hundred people in the large hall and twenty-five or thirty were crowded at the head of the stairs, either debating whether to go in or wishing they could go in if they had the admission.

Two middle-aged men stood in the doorway. White bands on their arms had the word 'Committee' printed on in blue letters.

Johnny gave one of the men two dollars and received four tickets that were promptly taken up by the other committeeman. They entered the dance hall and the first person Johnny saw was Karl Kessler, dancing with a plump flaxen-haired woman of about forty.

Kessler's eyes widened in astonishment.

He stopped dancing, said something to the woman and she walked off. Kessler came over.

"Surprised seeing you two here," he said, addressing Johnny and Sam. Then he nodded to Nancy. "Hello, Nancy."

"Hello, Karl," Nancy said, "meet my roommate, Jane Ballard."

"Pleasetameetcha," said Karl. He turned back to Johnny. "Didn't expect you at a German-Hungarian dance . . . "

"Oh, is that what this is?"

"It's the Clybourn Turnverein — athletic club, you know. This is their gymnasium week days."

"You're a member of the club?"

Kessler grimaced. "Me? I get enough exercise at the factory."

The music stopped and the dancers left the floor, but Johnny's group remained in a little huddle. Sam nudged Johnny and, when he caught his eye, nodded to someone at the right of the floor.

Carmella Vitali, surrounded by several dark-complexioned young men and a couple of Italian girls, was watching Johnny with a fierce scowl on his features.

"Oh-oh, the Black Hand's landed!"

Karl Kessler looked off. "Yah," he snorted. "Them punks come up here sometimes. Get drunk, pick fights with decent people. That Carmella's the worst one of the bunch."

"Might as well be at the factory," cut in Nancy Miller. "Who else is here we know?"

Kessler shrugged. "Three-four people. After all, there's six hundred people at the factory and most of them live on the north side. You're bound to meet some of them around here."

"I had a different idea," Nancy said, meaningly.

"In time, Taffy," Johnny said, jovially. "Say, d'you mind? I've got to make an important phone call . . . "

"Oh, go right ahead," said Nancy. "There're only about fifty stags here and I'll make out all right."

"You always make out all right, huh, Nancy?" asked Kessler, winking jovially. "If I was three-four years younger, I make play for you myself."

"Keep the wolves away from her, Karl," said Johnny. "I'll be back in time for the next dance."

He had already spotted a sign, TELEPHONE, and headed in that direction, but when he got to the sign he saw an arrow underneath pointing into an adjoining room, a barroom. Johnny went in and found customers lined up four deep at a short bar. There was a phone booth at the side of the bar, fortunately empty, and Johnny entered.

He closed the door, drowning out most of the noise from the bar, and dropped a nickel into the slot. He dialed the night number of the Wiggins Detective Agency.

Wiggins' wheezing voice came on: "Wiggins talking."

"Johnny Fletcher calling. I thought you were going to pull off Begley?"

"Why, I couldn't do that, Mr. Fletcher," replied Wiggins. "The customer paid for a job and I've got to — "

"He paid until when?" Johnny cut in.

"Well, midnight."

"All right," snapped Johnny, "I'm glad you're conscientious, anyway. Now, what have you got for me so far?"

"Quite a lot. Al Piper was married, three children. Owned his own home,

222

rather nice place on West Grace Street, worth around $15,000 to $18,000. No trouble with his wife, as far as my operator could find out. Mrs. Piper has taken it badly. She insists he had no enemies . . . "

"He had one enemy," Johnny interrupted. "The person who killed him."

"You're so right, Mr. Fletcher," wheezed Wiggins. "And as far as that goes, a wife never knows what her husband does away from home. Mrs. Piper thought her husband the soul of propriety, but my operator got an entirely different picture of Piper, away from home. He was a boozer, a fighting boozer. Picked quarrels with strangers. There was a place on Lincoln, near Fullerton he had a fight with a man only last week . . . "

"Get the man's name?"

"No. He was a stranger in the tavern. Piper they knew. The bartender thought Piper knew the man, though. Said they sat at a table for a long time, talking and bickering, then suddenly Piper hit the other man in the face with a whiskey bottle. The other man knocked Piper down, kicked him in the stomach, then ran out before anyone could stop him."

"Get anything on Carmella Vitali?"

"He's got a police record. Quite a record. Twenty-eight years old and has been arrested nine times, the first time when he was only thirteen years old. Did six months in the parental school, but hasn't served any time since. Probation two different periods."

"What's he been arrested for mostly?"

"Hoodlumism, vagrancy. Assault and battery, five times. Got fined three times."

"Small stuff," said Johnny.

"Oh, don't underestimate him, Fletcher. One of those assault charges was pretty serious. The victim pulled through, but if somebody important hadn't put in a good word for him he'd have gone up for quite a spell."

"Who was it put in the plea for him?"

"Alderman Jensen, of the 22nd Ward. The man whose skull Carmella fractured refused to sign a complaint. Jensen got to him."

"Who was it?"

"Man named Havetler."

"Don't know him. Mmm, what about Towner?"

Wiggins was quiet for a moment. Then his voice came on, again apologetically, it seemed to Johnny. "That's the tough one, Mr. Fletcher. My man's still down at the star morgue. He's telephoned in a couple of times, but he hasn't given me one thing about Mr. Towner, that everyone in Chicago doesn't already know . . . "

"I told you *I* don't know a thing about him. You and the whole city may know Towner, but I don't. What's the dope on him?"

"He's a very rich man. His father started the business in 1884, first a tannery, then another, then the leather factory. Forty-nine per cent of the Algar Shoe Company, 51 per cent of the Transo Shoe Company, stuff like that. When he died, he left a net estate of around eleven million dollars."

"When was that?"

"Oh, quite awhile ago. Nineteen thirty."

"Harry Towner got the entire estate?"

"All except a few small bequests. But Harry Towner's done all right on his

225

own, don't worry about that. They say he's worth thirty millions today."

"In other words, he's lousy with money? But what about his personal life?"

"Married twice. Once to a showgirl when he was twenty. Father got it annulled. Then he married Harriet Algar of the Algar Shoe outfit. Two children, a son Elliott and a daughter, Linda."

"Extracurricular?"

"Huh? Oh, I see what you mean. Discreet, very discreet, if any. Newspapers wouldn't print such things, not about a man worth thirty million. Towner's a big man in this city, a big man."

"All right," said Johnny, "he's big. And I'm paying you big money. I'll call you again in an hour. I hope you've got more for me then than you've given me now."

"My operators are still at it, but it's getting late . . . "

"Keep them at it," snapped Johnny and hung up.

He opened the door of the phone booth and almost collided with Carmella Vitali, who moved up from the bar.

226

"Hi, pal," Carmella said, baring strong, white teeth. "Shooting any pool lately?"

"Not much," replied Johnny. He looked past Carmella at a pair of sleek, swarthy young men in pin-stripe suits who could have passed for twins. Both were chewing gum and grinning as they watched Johnny and Carmella. "Not in the mood tonight, Carmella. I've got a girl here — "

"Sure, I saw you come in. Nice girl, ain't she?"

"Yes."

"Good taste. Same as mine."

"What?"

"My girl. She broke a date with me tonight."

"Nancy Miller?"

"Yep. Kinda surprised you brought her up here. Nancy likes nice places. Good food. Champagne cocktails."

"We only dropped in for a few minutes."

"Nancy's idea?"

"Mine."

"Mmm, thought it mighta been hers. Grand kid, but likes to rub it in. Just a little bit, you know. I quit my job and she breaks a date. You know, keep a fella in line. Girls like fellas with steady jobs."

"Oh, you're so right, Carmella. Well, I guess I'd better not keep her waiting."

Johnny tried to step past Carmella, but the two sleek, swarthy men somehow moved up beside Carmella and blocked Johnny. Carmella grinned toothily.

"What's the hurry, pal? Nancy's dancing now with the old strawboss . . . "

"Kessler?"

"Yeah, sure, the bird who kept riding me at the factory. Old enough to be her father. Harmless. There's a little matter, I kinda hate to bring up. A buck you owe me. From last night."

"You put soap in that chalk."

"Naw, it was already in. We keep that piece for wise guys who come around, making bets."

"It isn't the money," said Johnny, "it's the principle."

"Sure, sure, what's that you said? You're so right. It ain't the principle, it's the money. So shell out, huh?"

Johnny looked longingly past the three men to the door leading into the dance hall. It was a long way. With the music

228

playing again, a shout might not even be heard in the other room.

He sighed heavily. "Suppose I gave you the dollar, what then?"

"One thing at a time. The buck first . . ."

Johnny shrugged and reached into his pocket. He drew out his packet of money, searched for and found a dollar bill. He creased it lengthwise and returned the rest of his money to his pocket.

"Here," he said. He held out the folded bill and as Carmella reached for it, Johnny let it fall from his fingers. Carmella grabbed automatically downwards and Johnny straightened him up with a terrific uppercut. In fact, Carmella's body didn't stop when it was straightened up. It went over backwards, crashing to the floor with a dull thud.

The two sleek, swarthy men stopped chewing their gum and stared at Johnny in blank amazement. Johnny circled around then, stepped over the unconscious Carmella, and walked into the dance hall.

18

IN the main room, he pushed through the fringe of onlookers and got to the edge of the dance floor. He caught sight of Sam dancing painfully with Jane Ballard and moved in and out among the dancers to them.

"Sam, do me a favor. Keep an eye on the barroom. Carmella's in there — "

"If he's looking for trouble, Johnny . . . "

"He looked — and he found it. But he may wake up and want some more. Janie . . . "

Jane Ballard stepped out of Sam's arms, smiled tantalizingly and moved into Johnny's arms. Sam frowned a little, then shrugged and headed in the direction of the bar.

"I've been waiting for this, Johnny Fletcher," said Jane.

"So've I. Where's Nancy?"

"Dancing with the old boy. Never mind Nancy for a while. Pay attention to me. I want to find out if you're as smart as they say."

"They?"

"Oh, Nancy's been talking about you, last night and again tonight, before you came."

"You said, 'they.'"

Jane nodded over Johnny's shoulder. "Uncle Karl was up at the apartment last night."

"Uncle Karl? Kessler's Nancy's uncle?"

"Didn't you know?"

"No." Johnny was silent for a moment. "They were talking about me?"

"And how! But then isn't everybody at the factory? You start work one day as a laborer and the next you're practically running the place. I suppose that's an exaggeration, but you were given some kind of promotion, weren't you?"

"I guess you could call it that."

"At a big salary increase?"

Johnny chuckled. "Now, don't tell me that's all you're interested in — how much money I make?"

"Frankly, Johnny, I'm quite interested in what you're earning. If you think I'm going to marry a man earning thirty-six dollars a week and do the laundry in the kitchen sink, you've got a good big think coming to you. I'll marry for love, sure, but I'm only going to fall in love with A: a man who's got plenty of money or, B: a man who's *making* money. Big gobs of it."

"I made five hundred bucks today, Janie."

"Now," said Jane, "the conversation is getting interesting. So what're we doing here at this dump?"

"A dance with Nancy and we're off — to spend money."

The music stopped and Johnny searched the floor for Nancy and Karl Kessler. He saw them across the room and, with Jane clinging to his arm, crossed to them. Nancy watched them approach, quite aware of Jane's clinging arm.

"Quite a long phone call you made," Nancy said coolly.

"I got delayed," replied Johnny. "Your b.f. Carmella wanted to talk to me. About you."

"He's a liar," snapped Nancy. "Whatever he said about me — "

"He didn't say much. He had kind of an accident. Hurt his mouth, I guess, so

232

he had to stop talking."

"You had a fight with him?"

"You can't call one punch a fight. Oh-oh, he's with us again."

Nancy's eyes quickly followed Johnny's in the direction of the barroom. Carmella and his two friends were emerging. Carmella was walking stiffly. Sam Cragg emerged from a clump of dancers and confronted Carmella. Johnny, across the room, saw Carmella talk volubly for a moment then skirt Sam and head for the door. Sam stood undecided, shrugged, and turned toward the dance floor.

Johnny disengaged himself from Janie's grip and took Nancy's elbow. The music struck up again and he moved away with Nancy onto the dance floor.

"At last," said Johnny, "alone."

"Except for five hundred people," retorted Nancy. "I saw Janie giving you the business. She's the biggest gold digger in Chicago. I'm going to have it out with her tonight, when we get home. Either she moves or I."

"Well," said Johnny cheerfully, "this is the first time in quite a while that I've had two girls fighting over me."

"I'm not fighting over you. The dame just can't resist making passes at a man."

"Or men at her."

Nancy sniffed. "Even Carmella. He came up to the apartment exactly twice and she made a play for him. She thinks I don't know they were out together Wednesday." She stopped. "Did you make a date with her?"

"I'm partial to taffy-colored hair."

She drew back from him and looked into his face. Johnny grinned. The annoyance that had been in Nancy's face the past half hour suddenly faded. "I still don't like double-dates," she said.

"Okay," said Johnny, "we'll try it alone tomorrow night."

"That," said Nancy, "is a date!"

They made a half circuit of the dance floor, Nancy dancing very close to Johnny. Then she searched his face again.

"Who'd you telephone?"

"Oh, just the detective agency."

He felt her body stiffen under his hand. "What?"

"The detective agency that's having me shadowed. I hired them to shadow the

234

man who's shadowing me."

"You *know* who's having you shadowed?"

"Of course. Fellow named Wendland."

"Linda Towner's fiancé?" exclaimed Nancy.

He nodded. "Know him?"

"He's come into the office a few times — with Linda. He — he's looked me over."

"He stopped with looking?"

"Well, he went a little further a couple of weeks ago. Asked me what I did with my evenings. I wasn't having any of that. If he couldn't come right out and ask for a date, I wasn't going to help him along. I told him I went to church every evening. Then Linda came out of her father's office and that was that."

"Reason Number 184 why I don't like Freddie Wendland," Johnny said. "Mmm, you didn't tell me that Karl Kessler was your uncle."

"You didn't ask me. It's no secret. Everybody at the plant knows it. He got me my job. He's the only family I've got. My mother died when I was four years old and Uncle Karl raised me . . . But why should Wendland be shadowing you?"

"That's why I'm having *him* shadowed; I'm trying to find out why. I never saw the man before yesterday."

"Johnny," said Nancy, "I don't understand you at all. You started to work at the factory yesterday, as a laborer. Today you're up to your neck in a murder mystery, with people shadowing you and all sorts of things happening to you."

"That's what a fellow gets when he doesn't mind his own business," said Johnny wryly.

"Why don't you . . . mind your own business?"

"Can't. It's a disease with me." He shuddered. "Now, you take your uncle and Hal Johnson, the foreman, at the plant. *They* mind their own business and they've been working thirty-nine years in one plant."

"What's wrong with that?"

"Nothing. For them. But I'm made different, I guess. A week in one place and I can't stand it any more."

"You've been two days at the Towner Leather Company. Does that mean you'll be leaving in another five days?"

"I'm going to let you in on a secret," said Johnny. "This job is the first one I've had since I was a boy. Oh, I work, pretty hard sometimes, too. But I work for myself. I'm a book salesman, the greatest book salesman in the world."

"Then why aren't you selling books now?" cried Nancy.

"Because I had a little bad luck. Rather, somebody else had bad luck. The publisher who supplies me with books was locked out by the sheriff. He couldn't send me any books — "

"Can't you get them anywhere else?"

"If I had money to pay for them, yes."

"But you said you were the greatest book salesman in the world. If you're that good, why don't you have enough money to pay for the books . . . ?"

"That," said Johnny, "is what's wrong with Johnny Fletcher. When he's got money he won't work. Oh, I've tried it. One year I worked hard. I made more money than the president of the United States. And I wound up at the end of the year with what I started.

237

Nothing. You see, there are people in this country who run night clubs, horse races and crap games. They always find the Johnny Fletchers . . . "

The music stopped and Johnny released Nancy. "For example, there are night clubs in Chicago. And Johnny Fletcher's in Chicago, with a couple of hundred dollar bills in his pocket. So — let's go . . . !"

Sam Cragg spied Johnny and came forward. "Johnny," he said, "that Carmella fellow and his friends have left the dance. But they are waiting downstairs . . . "

"How many friends?"

"Two."

"Suckers," said Johnny.

Janie Ballard came strolling up with Karl Kessler.

"Got enough slumming?" she asked.

"I've got one more phone call to make," said Johnny, "then I'm ready to leave. Don't start dancing; it'll only take me a minute."

He smiled at Nancy, nodded to Sam and headed for the barroom.

In the phone booth, he dialed the Wiggins Detective Agency. "Wiggins," began the detective, but Johnny cut him off.

"Where's Wendland tonight?"

"Wendland. I don't believe I — "

"Cut it out!" snapped Johnny. "I want to know where he is right now. Your man's shadowing me for him, and Wendland's calling in and asking for reports."

"But, Mr. Fletcher," protested Wiggins. "I never told you — "

"Where's Wendland?" snarled Johnny.

"At the Chez Hogan," Wiggins replied quickly. "He phoned in only a few moments ago."

"What did you tell him?"

"Only that you were at a dance hall Clybourn Avenue."

"All right," Johnny said curtly, "I'm going to the Chez Hogan myself. But first there are a couple of points I want to clear up. This first marriage of Harry Towner's — the one his father had annulled . . . what was the date on that?"

"I have it right here. Just a moment. Ah yes, October 16, 1921, that's the annulment . . . "

"And when did he remarry?"

"Mmm, let's see. January 1922, but I don't see —"

"Never mind. Just one thing more, something that's stuck in my mind since you told me about it. You said Al Piper owned his own home and that it was worth $15,000 to $18,000."

"Approximately. My operator's estimate . . ."

"More or less is good enough. How the devil could he buy his own home — one costing that much, on his thirty-six or thirty-eight dollars weekly pay?"

"Why, I thought you knew about that, Mr. Fletcher. Piper had a sideline — he took bets for Marco Maxwell, the bookie. He got five per cent, hot or cold."

Johnny groaned. "Why doesn't somebody tell me these things!"

"The police knew it yesterday. I thought you'd heard by now . . ."

"I didn't. Is there anything else I ought to know?"

"About Al Piper? Only that that's what Piper and that Italian boy, what's his name, Carmella, had their quarrel about. Carmella started taking horse bets and

240

Piper got sore about it."

"Oh, fine," said Johnny. "Now you tell me. Is there any other important little trifle that I ought to know and don't?"

"About who?"

"About anyone connected with Piper's murder."

"Who's connected with it?"

"Anyone who worked at the Towner factory."

"You only paid me to investigate — "

"Oh, hell," broke in Johnny, "forget it. I'll call you later." He slammed the receiver on the hook and left the booth and the barroom.

Sam and the girls were waiting for him at the exit. Nancy regarded Johnny suspiciously as he came up but made no comment.

They started down the stairs. Halfway down Johnny said:

"This Carmella lad learns the hard way."

Carmella stood at the bottom of the stairs with his two pin-stripe-suited friends. Sam drew a deep breath. "This is my department, Johnny." He stepped ahead of Johnny.

"Hiya, fellas," he greeted Carmella and his friends as he hurried down the stairs.

"Hello, Ape," retorted Carmella, stepping back. The movement formed a V: Carmella at the point, his two friends, one on either side of the corridor, making the prongs of the V.

Sam grinned hugely and stepped into the V. The two sleek men promptly closed in, each gripping one of Sam's arms with both hands. Sam chuckled. "You fellas kiddin'?"

"See if this is kidding," snarled Carmella, swinging a vicious blow at Sam. The fist would have hit Sam in the face except that he suddenly ducked his head and took the blow on his skull. Carmella cried out in pain and danced back, shaking his bruised hand. Then Sam, with a sharp, sudden movement brought both of his arms out in front of his body. The two pugs were jerked forward. Sam pulled his arms free of their grips, snaked one arm about each dark head and cracked the two together. Both men cried out in agony and Sam pushed them away. One went down to his knees and gripped his head in both of his hands. The other man reeled against the wall, ricocheted from it and fell to the floor on his face.

Johnny, coming down with the girls, took their arms. "Watch your step, girls."

Sam followed Carmella who was backing away from him. "I got a little present for you too, greaseball," Sam said.

"Don't!" cried Nancy Miller. "Don't hit him."

Sam, surprised by this appeal, half turned. And then Carmella reached to his hip pocket and brought out a leather-covered blackjack. He sprang forward, the blackjack high over his head. Johnny, seeing Sam's peril, cried out in alarm.

"Sam — duck!"

Sam whirled back to Carmella, but was too late. The blackjack struck him on the head, just over his forehead. It made a dull, sickening thud.

Sam grunted in pain and staggered back. Carmella raised his hand again. Sam ducked, groped out for Carmella and caught him by the shirt front. But that didn't stop the Italian. His blackjack came down again and Sam fell to his knees. He carried a piece of Carmella's shirt front with him.

Johnny, blocked by Sam, tried hurdling his friend. He caught his foot on Sam, plunged headlong against Carmella and sent him staggering back. He clawed at Carmella's leg, tried to upset him and then — then lightning struck his head and shot through his entire body. It was followed by utter blackness.

19

THE bouncing of the car on rough pavement sent streaks of pain darting through Johnny's body. He groaned once or twice, flailed with his hands, then an especially nasty bump caused him to cry out.

"Cut it out!" he gasped. He sat up. A foot was planted into his face and pushed him back to the carpeted floorboard.

"Shuddup!" snarled a harsh voice.

With a rush, full consciousness returned to Johnny. He was lying almost doubled up on the floor between the rear and front seat of a limousine. Two men sat on the rear seat, their feet carelessly deposited on him.

"Get your foot out of my stomach," Johnny complained.

It was the wrong thing to say. A heel ground into his stomach and another foot kicked him in the side. "You'll talk big right to the end," a voice sneered; the voice of Carmella Vitali.

Johnny was silent a moment as the full gravity of his predicament penetrated his aching brain. Then he asked quietly: "Where's Sam Cragg?"

"In the hospital, for all we care," said Carmella nastily. "We didn't figure it necessary to bring him along."

Johnny groaned inwardly. The last he had seen of Sam he was on his knees after having taken two vicious blows with the blackjack. Johnny himself had taken only one blow and passed out. Yes, Sam probably was in the hospital. And Johnny . . ."

"Where are we?" he asked.

"Guess," said a strange voice.

"Out in the country," Johnny hazarded.

"Smart boy," said Carmella. "You ain't even lookin' and you figured that out."

"We haven't passed any street lights," retorted Johnny. "And we're on a paved road, bumpy, but we haven't made any stops and haven't crossed any streetcar tracks. That's the country."

"And you're right, Fletcher, dead right, although you'll probably be more dead than right in a few minutes. In fact,

I think this is as good a spot as any . . . Luigi!"

"Yeah, Carmella," replied the voice of the man in the front seat.

"Pull up."

Brakes squealed and the car came to a bumping stop. Feet stepped on Johnny, kicked him and the right car door was opened. Carmella got out of the car.

"All right, Fletcher."

Johnny turned and on all fours crawled out of the car. Carmella helped him the last part by grabbing his coat collar and yanking him. Johnny spilled to the gravelly road shoulder. A foot kicked him and he got heavily to his feet. By that time the other two men had gotten out of the car and all three faced Johnny. Johnny's head ached terribly, his body was a mass of bruises and aches, but the peril of his position brought Johnny erect and alert.

"Now, wait a minute, Carmella," he said quickly. "Let's talk this over. I've got some money . . . "

"You *had* some money," said Carmella. "You haven't got a nickel . . . "

"I can get some more."

"Not in Chicago you can't. Because when we get through with you, you won't be going back to Chicago. You been stickin' your nose into things that ain't none of your business. You been botherin' *me* and when someone bothers me . . . "

Carmella didn't finish the sentence. He swung with his fist at Johnny's face. Johnny rolled with the punch and received only a glancing blow, but he promptly fell to his knees and from there to his face.

"Get up," snarled Carmella. "I hardly hit you." He put the toe of a foot into Johnny's side and turned him over on his back. One of the two sleek, swarthy men stooped, caught Johnny's coat front in a fist and yanked him up to his knees. Johnny let his body remain limp.

A fist smashed into his face. Johnny suppressed a groan, but jerked himself free of the fist and fell on his back. He rolled over, covering his head as best he could with his arms.

They lifted him again, but Johnny remained limp, even under the savage blows that were rained on him. They finally let him fall, kicked him several times, then believing him unconscious they climbed into the car. The motor was started, the car went ahead a short distance, then was turned and began coming back. Headlights picked out Johnny on the left shoulder of the road. It took his entire will power to remain motionless as the car swerved toward him. But at the last moment the driver jerked the wheel to the right and the car roared past.

Johnny waited until the motor was a faint drumming. Then he gathered himself slowly together and struggled to his knees. He remained in that position a long time before he finally got to his feet. He looked around then and saw that he was on a road lined with trees that came close to the pavement. The moon was almost full and lighted up the road nicely, but Johnny saw no sign of habitation. Wait . . . ahead and to the right was a glow in the sky. That could be a town.

Johnny started walking. He went a hundred yards and suddenly became aware that a car was approaching from the rear. Quickly he stepped off the pavement to the road shoulder, scrambled through a shallow ditch and took refuge in the trees beyond.

The headlights swooped down, became a car that roared past. When the taillights had disappeared Johnny emerged from the woods.

He walked for a half mile and came to a crossroad, a paved road somewhat wider than the one on which he had been traveling. Lights flickered in the distance. Johnny turned into the road.

He went at least a mile before he came to a street light; another was a hundred yards beyond. Ten minutes walking brought him to a road sign: *Hillcrest City Limits*.

Hillcrest! The name struck a chord in Johnny's brain. Of course — this was the home of Harry Towner. Johnny started swiftly into the town. He passed a closed gas station, a few houses, then a store or two and two more closed gas stations. But there were cars on the street now and in another block he saw the bright lights of an all-night gas station.

An attendant was hosing down the driveway. Behind him, in the lighted station, was a wall clock. One-fifteen a.m. The attendant watched Johnny approach.

"I'm looking for Harry Towner's place," Johnny said. "Do you know where he lives?"

The man looked at Johnny suspiciously. "You kidding?"

"No, I'm not. I had an accident back a ways and I know I look like hell, but I've got to get to Towner's place."

"This time of the night?"

"This time of the night."

The man shrugged. "Right through town, three miles, turn right a mile, then left about a half. Big stone wall, big iron gate with an arch over it. Name *Five Knolls* on the arch. That's the place."

"Almost five miles!" exclaimed Johnny. "I can't walk that far."

"Probably wouldn't do you any good if you did," said the gas station attendant.

"Have you got a phone here I can use?"

"Pay phone inside."

Johnny went through his pockets. Carmella had told the truth. He had been stripped of every bill and coin in his pockets, in fact every scrap of paper.

251

Even his handkerchief had been taken from him.

"I haven't got a nickel," said Johnny. "I wonder if you'd — "

"No," said the attendant. "I'm a working man. I can't afford to give money to bums."

"I'm not a bum," said Johnny. "I was held up and robbed."

"I was held up myself, last week," retorted the attendant. "And believe me, the bonding company gave me a workout. Seemed to think I tapped the till."

"A nickel," said Johnny. "It won't break you. I want to phone Harry Towner. He'll send a car out after me."

"Yah!" jeered the attendant. "He'll send a car out at one-thirty in the morning; he will in a pig's ear. This is my home town and I know plenty about Harry Towner. He buys his gas from a truck; keeps a couple of tanks on the place. Saves a nickel a gallon that way."

"I work for Towner," Johnny persisted. "His leather factory in Chicago. He offered me the job of sales manager only yesterday."

252

"Sales manager, huh? You ain't doin' such a good sellin' job right now. You can't even talk me out of a nickel. You know what I think? Your face is full of blood and your clothes is all torn; I think you got thrown off a freight train."

"The hell with you!" snarled Johnny and started to walk off. He went twenty feet and then the man called out: "Hey, come back, here's your nickel."

Johnny turned and walked back. He took the nickel the man held out, started for the filling station. The attendant followed him.

"If you're on the level, call Hillcrest 1234; that's the local cab company. Ride out to Towner's and get him to pay for the cab."

Johnny took the receiver off the hook, hesitated, then dropped the nickel into the slot.

Five minutes later, a yellow taxicab pulled into the filling station and Johnny got in. He waved to the gas station attendant and leaned back against the leather cushions. "Five Knolls," he told the driver. "Harry Towner's place."

The man turned completely around in

his seat. "This time o' night — the way you look?"

"I had a car accident," Johnny said.

The driver hesitated, then muttered something to himself and turned away. The cab roared out of the gas station. It rolled through a village, headed for the country road beyond and a few minutes later drove up to an ornamental iron gate. Worked into the archway overhead were the words Five Knolls.

The driver got out, came around and opened the cab door for Johnny. "Two seventy-five," he said.

"Pretty steep for five miles," Johnny objected.

"Night rates — and I got to go back."

Johnny pointed to the gates. "Ring for the bell, will you?"

"Why?"

"Well, if you must know, I haven't got any money with me."

The cabby stepped to the front door, opened it and reaching in brought out a big wrench. "All right," he said, "I'll get no money out of it, but I'll get satisfaction. You'n me are taking a ride to the jailhouse."

254

Johnny stepped around the cabby and moved backwards to the big iron gate. He found the bell at the side of it and pressed long and hard.

"Give me five minutes," he said to the cabby, who had followed him with the wrench, held poised for striking. "If I don't get the money for you, I'll go with you quietly."

He pressed the bell again. There was a cottage just inside the gate and after a moment, a light went on in it. Johnny pressed the bell a third time. A door opened, framing a man in undershirt and trousers. "Who is it?" he called.

"I want to see Mr. Harry Towner," Johnny called back.

"What's the name?"

"Fletcher."

The man in the cottage doorway shook his head. "Mr. Towner didn't tell me about any Fletcher calling in the middle of the night."

"He didn't expect me to call."

"Then I'm afraid you'll have to wait until morning."

"If you make me wait until morning," Johnny said grimly, "I can assure you

you'll lose your job. This is a matter of life and death. Phone the house and tell Mr. Towner that Johnny Fletcher is here with important information about the murder at the plant."

"The murder!" exclaimed the gatekeeper.

"You heard me."

The man hesitated then, leaving the door open, went back into his cottage. Johnny could see him cross to a wall phone, take down the receiver and wait a moment. Then he pressed a button. He waited for a long moment, spoke into the phone, waited and spoke again. Then he hung up and came out of the cottage.

He waddled up to the gate, shot back a bolt and pulled the gate open a foot or so. "Mr. Towner says to come up, but it better be good. That's what he said."

"It'll be good," said Johnny. "Now, give this taxi driver five dollars."

"What for?" cried the gatekeeper.

"Look at me," said Johnny sternly. "I was waylaid and robbed on my way out here. I haven't got a nickel in my pocket. Give the man the five dollars; you'll get it back from Mr. Towner in the morning." He turned to the cabby. "Okay?"

The man lowered his wrench. "Okay, chum . . . Want me to wait?"

"No," said Johnny, "I'll be spending the night here."

He nodded, stepped through the aperture in the gate and started up a winding drive to the huge shadow of the house, a hundred yards or more from the gate.

A light was on in an upper room and as Johnny approached lights went on downstairs. When he got to the door it was already opened and a servant in a bathrobe greeted him.

"Mr. Fletcher? Mr. Towner is in the library."

Johnny entered and the butler led him through a wide hall to a room at the rear, an immensely large room with thousands of books on the shelves, most of them in leather bindings, most of them as untouched as the day they had been bound.

Harry Towner was pacing before a massive teakwood desk, a cold cigar champed in his mouth. He stopped when Johnny entered the room.

"What happened to you?" he cried when

he noted Johnny's physical appearance.

"I was taken for a ride," said Johnny, "and left for dead."

Towner's eyes widened in shock. "Who did it?"

"A man named Carmella Vitali . . . "

"That Italian the police questioned?"

"Yes."

Towner whirled to his desk, scooped up a phone.

"No," said Johnny quickly. "Don't call the police. I want him to think I'm dead and tomorrow I'll nail him. Good."

"At least, let me call a doctor. You look like hell, Fletcher."

"I haven't got any broken bones," said Johnny. "I look worse than I feel." That was a lie. "But I'd like to take a hot shower and get some sleep."

"Cedric!" roared Towner. The butler in the bathrobe popped into the library. "Show Mr. Fletcher to a room. Run a hot bath for him and do whatever else you can."

"Thanks," said Johnny wryly. He followed the butler out of the room, climbed a stairs and proceeded down a wide carpeted hall.

The butler opened a door, switched on lights and Johnny entered a bedroom about half as large as the Northwestern Depot. The bathroom was as big as the average two-room apartment and had a square tub in which you could execute naval maneuvers. Johnny peeled off his clothes while the butler ran hot water into the tub.

"I can handle the rest," Johnny said. "Thanks."

"Very well, sir," said the butler. "Should you want medication or, ah, bandages, you'll find them in the medicine cabinet."

Johnny soaked himself in the tub for fifteen minutes, then got out, dried himself and, naked, crawled into the huge bed. He didn't bother turning out the lights.

20

JOHNNY was awake, feeling his bruises, when there was a knock on the bedroom door. "Yes?" he called.

The door opened and Elliott Towner came into the room. "We're driving into town in a half hour," he said, coming forward. "Dad wanted me to find out if you're in condition to go in with us."

"I will be, after I eat some breakfast," exclaimed Johnny. He threw back the covers and leaped out of bed, wincing as bruised muscles protested.

Elliott looked at Johnny's torn, soiled suit lying on the floor beside the bed. "You could wear a suit of mine. We're about the same size."

"Now," cried Johnny, "that's decent of you."

Elliott left the room and Johnny went into the bathroom. When he came out, a suit and a clean shirt were lying on the bed. Johnny put them on and left the room.

He descended to the main floor and a maid directed him to the breakfast room, where the entire Towner clan, the Leather Duke, Linda and Elliott were all seated at a table, eating breakfast.

"Feel all right?" Harry Towner asked.

Johnny nodded. "Fine. Good morning, Miss Towner."

"I've just been hearing about your latest, Johnny," said Linda, "and I think you're a liar. You don't look fine and you aren't fine. In fact, you look like something the cat dragged in."

Johnny grinned wryly, saw a phone on the sideboard and crossed to it. "Operator," he said into the mouthpiece. "I want the Lakeside Athletic Club in Chicago." He covered up the mouthpiece. "Excuse me, but I'm worried about my friend, Sam Cragg. We got separated last night."

An operator said in his ear: "Lakeside Athletic Club."

"Suite 512," Johnny said, "Mr. Cragg."

Thirty seconds passed and then the voice said: "I'm sorry, Mr. Cragg does not answer."

"Try 514, the adjoining room."

"I've rung both, sir. Do you wish to leave a message?"

Johnny hung up. "Something happened to Sam."

"That's the man who lifts two hundred pound barrels," said the Leather Duke. "What could happen to him?"

"I don't know, but the last time I saw him he was down on his knees and a man was hitting him with a blackjack . . ."

The entire Towner family stared at Johnny. He drew a deep breath. "Your switchboard operator was watching, Mr. Towner . . . Nancy Miller . . ."
Johnny's eyes shifted quickly to Elliott Towner.

Elliott's mouth was open wide enough to swallow a duck egg.

"Fletcher," said the Leather Duke. "Sit down and have your breakfast. Then we'll ride into town and clear up this whole mess. I think a few people at the factory are going to find themselves without jobs."

"Oh, I say," protested Elliott. "You can't just fire people like that." He looked hard at Johnny. "On someone's unsubstantiated accusation."

"Accusation?" asked Johnny. "I didn't accuse anyone."

"You just said, at least you intimated, that this girl, what's her name — Nancy Milton? — was involved."

"The name is Miller," Johnny said, "M-i-l-l-e-r, the same as the girl called you at the club night before last."

"What?" cried Elliott Towner.

"The girl who told you she knew who killed Al Piper . . . "

Elliott Towner kicked back his chair, sprang to his feet. His face was a picture of utter consternation. Harry Towner banged his fist on the breakfast table.

"What's this, Elliott?"

"He's a liar," Elliott cried, hoarsely. "I — I don't know what he's talking about."

"Nancy Miller," said Johnny, "she telephoned you eight times at the Lakeside Athletic Club in one evening. You were there, but wouldn't take the calls. Then she tried to break into the club and go up to your room. They stopped her in the lobby. She phoned again after that and — well, the operator made a mistake and put her through . . . "

Elliott's face went from consternation to abject horror, or terror.

"Fletcher," he began thickly. "I — I've had about all I can take from you . . . "

"Elliott," the Leather Duke said, sternly, "I want a direct answer — just a yes or no. Did this girl telephone you at the club?"

Elliott took a step away from the table, but reeled and had to reach out to the chair to support himself.

"Answer me!" snapped Harry Towner.

"Y-yes."

Linda Towner suddenly interrupted. "Just a minute, Dad." She turned to Elliott. "You're in love with Nancy, aren't you?"

"No!" exclaimed Elliott.

"But you've taken her out?" Linda paused a moment, waiting for a denial and when it did not come, went on: "She's blackmailing you, isn't she?"

With a tremendous effort Elliott pulled himself together. He gave Johnny a bitter glance and started from the room. Harry Towner pushed his chair away from the table. "Elliott," he roared. "I want the truth of this."

"I'm sorry, Dad," said Elliott, doggedly, "I can't tell you . . . " He continued on out of the room.

Harry Towner glared at the empty doorway, then whirled and glowered at Johnny. "Do *you* know the truth?"

"No," said Johnny. "Not all of it."

"But Elliott's really involved with that girl?"

"To a certain extent, yes."

"You made several rather exact statements — eight phone calls in one evening. How did you get that information?"

"By using some of your money, Mr. Towner, and sticking my nose into other people's business."

"At that you're very good," snapped Towner. "Yesterday you had a mouse on your cheekbone, today your own mother wouldn't recognize you. I'm curious as to how you'll look tomorrow."

"No worse," said Johnny, "because I'm going to wind this up today." He added drily, "I've got to, because I can't take another beating. I want to make just one more phone call . . . "

"While you're making it, I'll get ready."

Harry Towner left the breakfast room and Johnny stepped again to the phone.

He gave the operator the number of the Wiggins Detective Agency, then looked over the phone at Linda Towner who had not left the room.

Wiggins came on the wire. "Wiggins Detective Agency," he wheezed.

"I thought you had a man shadowing me last night?" Johnny snarled. "You bragged that he was the best shadower in the detective business — "

"Mr. Fletcher!" cried Wiggins. "How are you?"

"Lousy!"

"I was afraid of that, Mr. Fletcher. Uh, Begley went to telephone the police when those hoodlums assaulted you last night. When he came back you were, ah, gone . . . So he, ah, shadowed your friend, Sam Cragg . . . "

"What happened to Sam?"

"Why, ah, nothing. He was knocked out for a few minutes, but someone threw some water on him and he got up."

"But he didn't go home last night. I just telephoned the club and he wasn't there."

"No, he wouldn't be. You see he, ah, spent the night at an apartment on, ah, Armitage . . . "

"What?" cried Johnny. Then he suddenly chuckled. "I'll be damned."

Wiggins proceeded: "As a matter of fact, he just left a half hour ago. He's now in the factory of the Towner Leather Company and my man's outside."

"Okay," said Johnny. "I'll be there myself inside of an hour."

"Very good. But, Mr. ah, Fletcher, I have some information for you."

"About who?"

"The man with the Italian name, Carmella . . . "

"I hope it's good," Johnny said, grimly.

"Oh, it's quite good. I mean bad. It seems that he wore a tan work shirt the day before yesterday, when the, ah, tragedy occurred at the leather factory. Well, my man found that shirt in the bottom of a garbage can behind Carmella's place of residence. It contains bloodstains . . . "

"Human blood?" cried Johnny.

"As far as we could tell. As a matter of fact, the shirt's in my office right now. I have some interesting information about the dead man. His salary was approximately thirty-eight dollars and fifty cents a week, yet he banked an average of one hundred dollars a week, for the past six years. I think that is very significant, Mr. Fletcher, inasmuch as there are approximately six hundred employees at the leather factory and certainly not more than five per cent would wager on horses . . . "

"Guess again," said Johnny. "Fifty per cent would be nearer the truth. What else?"

"I have a rather complete thumbnail biography of Mr. Towner."

"Give it to me — at least the salient features."

"This is highly libelous, as a matter of fact, it was never printed in the papers, for that very reason. My man got it from the custodian of the *Star* morgue, an old man, who was a reporter on the *Star* in his younger days. It, ah, pertains to the late *Mrs*. Towner."

"Number one or two?"

"Oh, two. The first was never really referred to as Mrs. Towner. In fact, as far as the public press is concerned, there has always been only one Mrs. Towner."

"All right, get to the point, man."

"I will. As I said, this is highly libelous and at this late date would be almost impossible to verify."

"Get to the point, Wiggins!"

"I'm trying to tell you, Fletcher. Shortly after the marriage, Mrs. Towner went away. To Europe. Her child was born there, young Elliott."

"Well?"

"That's it, Mr. Fletcher. She was gone a year and when she brought the child back, well, he seemed rather, shall we say, large for his age?"

Johnny looked over the phone again, at Linda Towner, who was sitting at the breakfast table, moodily poking at a half grapefruit, with a spoon. He nodded thoughtfully.

"Thank you, Wiggins. I — I'm just leaving for the plant now . . . with Mr. Towner."

Wiggins' wheeze almost blasted Johnny's eardrum. "You mean you're telephoning from *his* house?"

"Yes, good-bye."

He started to put down the receiver, then raised it back to his ear. Wiggins' click came over the phone, then another. Someone in the Towner residence had been listening in on an extension phone.

Johnny put down the receiver and headed for the door. Linda Towner pushed back her chair. "I'm going to the office with you."

"It's all right with me, Linda," Johnny said, quietly. "If you'll tell me why Freddie Wendland had me shadowed all day yesterday . . . "

"Freddie?"

"The detective who followed us to lunch and back — Wendland was paying for him."

"That's ridiculous!" cried Linda. "There's no earthly reason why Freddie should — "

"Jealousy?" suggested Johnny. Linda stared at him. "You went to the Chez Hogan with him last night."

"Yes, but . . . " Linda looked suspiciously at him. "How did you know?"

"The detective I was just talking to on the phone, that's the one Wendland hired. Well, I paid him more money than Wendland did."

"So you've been spying on Freddie!"

"In a small way."

Harry Towner appeared in the doorway. "If you're ready, Fletcher."

"I'm ready."

"I'll just get my coat," exclaimed Linda. "Take me only a second . . . "

She ran past her father. Towner looked after her. Johnny said: "She wants to go into town with us."

"I'd rather she didn't."

"I'd just as soon she did," Johnny said. "Fred Wendland's mixed in this business."

"That tired old college boy?" Towner snorted. "If he ever becomes my son-in-law, I'll send him down to manage my Nashville Tennessee tannery. I don't think I could stand him around here."

He started out of the room. Johnny followed. Before they reached the front door, Linda came running up, carrying a tweed coat.

A big limousine was standing in the driveway before the house. A uniformed chauffeur stood by the tonneau door.

"Elliott leave?" Harry Towner asked.

"A moment ago," the chauffeur said. "He took the yellow convertible."

Towner grunted. "Fine thing to break down the morale of the hands. Come to work in a Cadillac, an hour and a half late."

He stepped into the Lincoln Continental.

21

IT was shortly after nine-thirty when Harry Towner, his daughter Linda and Johnny entered the offices of the Towner Leather Company.

Nancy Miller was at the switchboard, her face somewhat pale and strained even under heavier than normal makeup. Harry Towner, in the lead, gave her a curt nod. Linda, coming next, smiled sweetly. "Good morning, Nancy."

Johnny said: "Hi, Taffy, you're looking like a million."

Nancy only stared at Johnny.

Johnny went to the elevator, which was waiting at the first floor and rode up to the fifth floor. He stepped out and began strolling leisurely through the flat counter department, the gluing department and the molding machines until he reached the counter sorting department.

Hal Johnson was leaning against his high desk, his back to the sorters, and looking gloomily down the line of molding machines.

His eyes flickered over Johnny's battered features. "Got a good one this time," he commented.

"A beauty," admitted Johnny.

"Johnny!" boomed the voice of Sam Cragg. He came pelting down the aisle. Johnny moved to meet him. Sam skidded to a halt and stared at Johnny.

"Carmella worked you over, Johnny! I'll kill 'im."

"I may let you do just that, Sam." Johnny sized up Sam. "You don't look any the worse."

"Me? Heck, that wasn't nothing. I hadda kind of lump on the old noggin, but Janie . . . " He suddenly coughed and looked past Johnny at Johnson.

"I know all about it, Sam," said Johnny grinning. "You spent the night at the girls' apartment."

"Yeah, Johnny, but don't get no wrong ideas. Janie wanted me to come up and put some cold compacts on the bean, then, well, I, uh, she thought I'd better stay there in case I needed more treatments. I — I slept on the couch."

"Sure, Sam, it's all right."

"On'y I couldn't sleep much on accounta worrying about you, Johnny."

"I spent the night out at the Duke's house."

Hal Johnson heard that. "You spent the night at the Towner estate? Thirty-nine years I've worked for him and I've never even seen the layout. Forty-eight hours ago you hadn't even met Harry Towner."

"Well," said Johnny, "the food's lousy at the Towner house. I mean, they didn't even give me any breakfast." He grinned feebly. "Being a pal of the Duke's has some drawbacks . . . about seventy-five, I'd say. All over my body. I think two of my ribs are cracked." He nodded down the department. "I see Elliott's on the job, this morning."

"Came in ten minutes ago," said Johnson.

Johnny's eyes fell upon Cliff Goff, the horseplayer. "Just a minute," he said to Sam and Johnson. He strode away from them, to Goff.

The horseplayer was sorting counters. He was looking at them, but he wasn't seeing them. His mind was miles away, riding with Arcaro at Pimlico, or Skoronski at Arlington, or Longden at Santa Anita.

Johnny tapped him on the shoulder. Goff exclaimed, shook his head and looked at Johnny.

"I want to put two bucks on a horse," Johnny said, "who'll I give the bet to?"

"Oh, Al," said Goff, automatically, then grimaced. "Al's dead."

"He owe you any money?"

"No, I owed him. Fourteen dollars."

"Thanks," said Johnny and walked back to Johnson and Sam.

"Al Piper was the factory bookie," Johnny said to the foreman.

"Who says so?" Johnson demanded.

"*I* said so," retorted Johnny.

"I don't know what you're talking about."

"Not officially, no, but no employee could take horse bets around here for more than two days without the foreman knowing about it."

"I don't know anything about it," Johnson persisted. "But I don't see why it should make any great difference. You can't keep people from betting on horses.

They'd sneak out and make bets, or an outside bookie'd be sneaking in all the time. Somebody on the inside books a few quarters or half dollars, what difference does it make?"

"None to me," said Johnny. "Personally, I've sent a few bookies' sons to Harvard and a few daughters to Vassar and Smith."

"You're going to snitch to Towner?"

"Tell me just one thing — and this I *can* and *will* prove. Was Al Piper cutting you in for a percentage, for the privilege of taking bets?"

"No," said Johnson bluntly.

"But he was paying *some*one?"

Hal Johnson did not answer that. Johnny shook his head. "You know that Carmella was trying to muscle in on the business?"

"The hell with Carmella," snarled Johnson. "And the hell with you, Fletcher." He started to turn away, but whirled back. "And you," stabbing a thick forefinger at Sam Cragg. "If you're working here, get back to your bench, or go down and draw your pay."

"I'm fired?" Sam asked, eagerly.

"Either I'm foreman here," Johnson said, doggedly, "or I'm not. You're fired."

"Great!" exulted Sam.

Johnson looked at Johnny. "Is he fired?"

"You're the foreman, Hal," Johnny said, quietly.

"All right, then he isn't fired."

"No!" howled Sam. "You can't go back on it. You said I was fired . . ."

"Ah," said Johnson in disgust and walked off.

Sam appealed to Johnny. "Let me be fired, Johnny. I feel silly sitting at a bench like this, squeezing them little hunks of leather. It ain't no kind of a job for a grown man."

Instead of replying Johnny stepped to Johnson's desk and picked up the phone. "Hi, Taffy," he said into the mouthpiece. "This is Johnny . . ."

"I'm sorry, Johnny," Nancy exclaimed. "I couldn't say anything with Mr. Towner present, but I — I'm terribly sorry about last night. What — what happened?"

"Nothing much," said Johnny. "I only got beaten within an inch of my life.

That I'm not dead isn't your boy friend's fault."

"Don't say that, Johnny. Carmella isn't my boy friend. He never has been."

"How about Elliott Towner?"

There was silence on the phone for a full second. Then Nancy said: "I don't know what you're talking about, Johnny . . . "

"A bellboy at the Lakeside Athletic Club," Johnny said, "night before last . . . "

This time there were two full seconds of silence before Nancy said: "You knew that — last night?"

"I knew. Wait, Nancy, it won't do you any good to try to leave the building. There's someone outside . . . "

"I have no intentions of leaving the building," Nancy Miller said, steadily. "I'm merely going to get back to my work . . . "

"Get me the police department," Johnny said. "Homicide Squad — Lieutenant Lindstrom . . . "

"Lieutenant Lindstrom is in Mr. Towner's office right now."

"Get him for me."

A moment later Lindstrom's voice

snapped: "Lindstrom talking."

"Fletcher up in the counter department. Get Carmella Vitali at once."

"Who's this?" exclaimed Lindstrom. "Commissioner Fletcher?"

"Johnny Fletcher, not Commissioner Fletcher."

"Oh, is that so? Well, le'me tell you something, Fletcher. I don't take orders — "

"That isn't an order," cut in Johnny, "but if you don't pick up Carmella Vitali, you'd better not read the newspapers this evening. And you'd better start looking over the vacation folders, because you'll be going on a good long suspension."

Johnny slammed down the receiver, then picked it up again. "Don't bother calling Carmella, Taffy!"

"Why you . . . " began Nancy Miller. Johnny hung up.

Sam Cragg came forward. "What'd you wanna have the cops pick up Carmella for, Johnny? I thought you'd let me have that pleasure. I wasn't really gonna kill him. Only halfway . . . "

"You may still get your chance." Johnny looked toward the rows of barrels

280

behind the counter department. "Sam, I want you to go back to the spot where Al Piper was found . . . "

Sam shuddered. "Aw, Johnny," he protested. "It's dark back there. I get the shivers when I even look . . . "

"This'll just be for a minute."

"What'd you want me to do?"

"Just stand there and call me — but not too loud. About like this: 'Say, Johnny.'"

Sam hesitated, then shaking his head went off. Johnny followed him for part of the distance, but when Sam cut into the aisle between the barrels Johnny continued down the line to Elliott Towner's bench.

Elliott watched him approach, his face dark and smoldering.

"Hi, Elly," Johnny said, as he came up.

"Keep away from me, Fletcher," Elliott snarled. "I'm in no mood for your — "

Behind the barrels, Sam Cragg called: "Hey, Johnny . . . !"

And then there was a tremendous crash!

Johnny gasped and started running

from a standing start. He reached the aisle leading to the rear of the barrels, hurtled down it and skidded into a left turn.

In several swift bounds he reached the death aisle. Sam Cragg was climbing over a heap of wreckage in the aisle, wood and several thousand counters scattered on the floor.

"Jeez, Johnny!" he cried. "Somebody gave this pile of barrels a shove from the other side. Almost hit me with them."

"I should have warned you, Sam," Johnny said, through clenched teeth.

"You knew somebody was gonna do it?"

"No, I didn't know, but I should have suspected it. Here . . . " He leaned over the wreckage, gave Sam his hand and helped him clear. When they reached the aisle, several spectators were looking in. Hal Johnson, Karl Kessler, Elliott Towner and two or three counter sorters.

"Somebody just tried to kill Sam," Johnny said, grimly. "They fixed up a pile of barrels so they could be pushed over easily . . . "

"You've been inviting it, Fletcher,"

snapped the foreman. "You hang around here much longer and somebody else will be killed."

"No," said Johnny. "I've had enough. I'm going to spill what I know — now. Down in Harry Towner's office. I think you ought to hear it, Hal. And you, Karl . . ." He nodded to Elliott. "And you, Elliott . . ."

"I'm not interested," Elliott Towner said.

"You'd better be. Come on, all of you . . ."

"He giving the orders now, Hal?" Karl Kessler asked, quietly.

"*I'm* giving the orders," cried Johnson. "And that's one of them. Downstairs to The Duke's — I mean, Mr. Towner's office . . ."

22

THE men from the counter department filed from the elevator into the office: Hal Johnson, the foreman, Karl Kessler, the assistant foreman, Elliott Towner, son of the factory owner, then Sam Cragg and last, Johnny Fletcher. In that formation they headed for Hal Johnson's private office.

Johnny paused at the switchboard. "The showdown, Taffy. Better join us."

"No," said Nancy Miller stubbornly.

Elliott Towner stepped out of the single file formation. "Let her alone," he said ominously.

"You're the boss's son," said Johnny, shrugging. He continued on after the others. But at the door of Towner's office he looked back. Nancy Miller was getting up from her switchboard desk. And as Johnny waited, she came forward.

Harry Towner watched the entry of

284

his visitors. In the office already were his daughter Linda and her fiancé, Freddie Wendland.

"What's this?" The Leather Duke asked. "A shop grievance committee?"

"The last act," Johnny said, "the finale, in which you will learn everything — well, almost everything. Remember what I said to you yesterday when I took on this job?"

"No," said Towner, "but Wendland's just been telling me some things about you . . ."

"Phooey on Freddie," said Johnny flippantly. "Mr. Wendland will sit in the corner and keep his mouth shut while his inferiors carry on."

Wendland cried out and started forward, but The Leather Duke waved his hand and Wendland swerved and went to a far corner of the room and seated himself.

Johnny looked around the circle of faces. "Well," he said, "does anyone want to make a confession and save us all time?"

No one in the room said a word.

Johnny nodded. "I thought not. You're

still hoping against hope that I'm nothing but a loud-mouthed fool." He drew a deep breath. "Mr. Towner, since everyone here is a member of the great big Towner leather family, you won't mind, I'm sure, if I wash a little dirty family linen."

"Go ahead, wash," said Harry Towner grimly, "but you'd better wash it clean, because I'll probably throw you out of this office on your ear when you get through."

"It's about your first marriage, Mr. Towner," said Johnny.

"Dad's only been married once," Elliott Towner cut in.

"Twice," Johnny corrected. "Of course, I guess he doesn't count the first one because it was annulled after only a few days. He married beneath his station, you know, a chorus girl or someone like that. A gold-digging chorus girl, with rather low morals . . . Did you say something, Karl?"

"I said you were a liar," Kessler said clearly. "A dirty, no-good, stinking liar. Elsie was — "

"Your sister?" Johnny asked quickly.

"What's that?" cried Harry Towner.

Johnny's eyes slitted. "You didn't know?"

"Of course not. Her name was Elsie King . . ."

"Her professional name. Before she went on the stage, it was Elsie Kessler."

Towner looked at Kessler in bewilderment. "But, Karl, you never breathed a word . . ."

"And lose my job?" Kessler asked bitterly. "Your father paid Elsie off. Five hundred dollars he gave her, for the child — "

"Child!" Towner cried hoarsely. "What child?"

"Your daughter."

"Nancy Miller," Johnny said quietly.

Harry Towner looked at Johnny, then stared for a moment at Karl Kessler. Then he suddenly strode across the room to where Nancy was standing stiffly just inside the door. He peered into her face for a long time. Then he slowly shook his head. "No," he said, "I don't believe it."

"And neither do I," Johnny said.

"I have birth certificate to prove

it," said Karl Kessler. "Also hospital records."

"I've seen them, Dad," suddenly said Elliott Towner.

"You?" cried The Leather Duke.

"I've known about it for months. I — I asked Nancy to marry me, then Karl, well Karl told me I couldn't, because she was my half sister."

"They really sold you that bill of goods, Elliott?" Johnny asked.

"I've seen the documents."

"You've seen some pieces of paper. And some old newspaper clippings about the first marriage and annulment. The newspaper clippings were real." Johnny paused. "And you were in love with Nancy." He laughed shortly. "Funny, how a man in love with a girl will believe every word she tells him. How much has it cost you, so far?"

Elliott Towner winced. His father saw it and came toward him. "Elliott, have you been giving money to these people?" He waited for his son to answer and when he didn't, he gripped his arm. "Answer me!"

"Yes," Elliott finally admitted miserably.

"They — I mean, he," indicating Karl, "said he'd been quiet long enough. He was going to tell the newspapers the whole story."

"But there isn't any story, son," exclaimed Harry Towner. "It's true I was married to a girl named Elsie King and that the marriage was annulled. My father — your grandfather — proved to me that she — "

"That's a lie!" cried Karl Kessler.

"All right," said Harry Towner, "let's say then that I was drunk when I married her. And *that's* true. I woke up in Lake Geneva one morning and discovered that I had a wife."

"And six months later, you married another woman who had to go to Europe to have her baby because — "

"*That*," said Harry Towner coolly, "*is* a lie!" He regarded Kessler steadily. "How long have you worked for this company?"

"Thirty-nine years, eight months and eleven days. A lifetime and now, in my old age, I am fired!"

"You're not fired," said Johnny, "you're just taking a leave of absence. Until

289

they take you down to Joliet for the execution . . . "

All eyes in the room were on Johnny. He looked steadily at Nancy Miller, then at Karl Kessler. "You let Al Piper have the bookie concession; for a weekly consideration, of course. You knew that, Hal, didn't you?"

Hal Johnson said nothing.

Johnny continued. "And then Carmella began going out with your niece, Karl, and *he* began taking bets. Al complained but you wouldn't do anything about it. Then Al, who knew quite a lot about you already, did a little nosing around — during his last binge. He found out about Elliott and Nancy — and the little blackmail job you were pulling. He came back to work two days ago and nailed you with it."

Lieutenant Lindstrom of Homicide appeared suddenly in the doorway. He pulled someone along from behind, a handcuffed Carmella Vitali.

"Ah," said Johnny. "I was just telling how Karl Kessler here cut Al Piper's throat . . . "

Nancy Miller screamed.

"I'm sorry, Taffy," said Johnny softly. "He's your uncle, all right, but then — but then, Elliott *isn't* your half brother. Maybe that'll make up."

"I had nothin' to do with it," suddenly yelped Carmella. "I seen him come out of the aisle with the bloody knife."

"You fool!" roared Karl Kessler. He suddenly reached under his apron and brought out an eight-inch leather knife, a knife as sharp as a razor and with a point like a needle. He lunged for Johnny. "You . . . !" he mouthed. "I'll take you . . . "

Sam took two quick strides forward. He came up beside Karl Kessler and hit him with his fist, in the back of the head. Karl Kessler plummeted clear across the room, his head striking the far wall. He dropped to the floor and remained still. And while all eyes were on him, Sam Cragg wheeled and slapped Carmella Vitali with his open palm. It was one of the hardest blows Sam had ever struck, and it was a cowardly blow, too, since Carmella was handcuffed and could not defend himself. But cowardly or not, the result was the same. Carmella

Vitali went into the same slumberland as Karl Kessler.

★ ★ ★

Some ten minutes later, Harry Towner's office contained only Harry Towner, Johnny and Sam, and Linda.

"Thirty-nine years, eight months and eleven days," said Harry Towner. "The man never had any other job in his whole life."

"And he was getting forty-five a week," Johnny said. "And getting old."

"Don't rub it in, Fletcher," said Harry Towner. "As a matter of fact, Elliott's been talking to me for months about a pension plan for employees. It's going to be put into effect as soon as I can work out the details with Elliott."

"You mean," said Sam, "if I work here I could get a pension?"

"Yes," said Johnny, "and you'd only have to work thirty-nine years . . ."

The phone on Towner's desk rang. He scooped it up, said: "Yes? Oh . . ." He held out the phone. "For you, Fletcher."

Johnny crossed and took the phone.

292

"Fletcher talking . . ."

"Wiggins," wheezed a voice. "I've got something for you. My operator — "

"Never mind," said Johnny, "the case is closed."

"Wait a minute," cried Wiggins. "This is personal . . . " He spoke for a moment and Johnny's face lit up. He said, "Thanks" and hung up. He looked at Sam and rubbed his hands together. "Wiggins' man lost me last night, Sam, so he began backtracking. He traced us back to the Eagle Hotel — "

"Ouch!" said Sam. "The flea-bag that evicted us two weeks ago . . . "

"The same joint," said Johnny, "hot cockroaches and running mice in every room. But it was home for us, Sam. And they've got a telegram there. From Mort Murray . . . He's out of hock, Sam, and sending us a shipment of books, prepaid. Get that, Sam, prepaid . . . !"

"We're back in the book business!" Sam beamed. "Then I don't have to work here for thirty-nine years?"

"That's right, Sam. We're free men."

"About that sales manager position, Fletcher," said Harry Towner. "The job

293

pays fifteen thousand a year . . . "

"Take it, Johnny Fletcher!" cried Linda Towner.

Johnny shook his head. "And see you coming in here to visit your husband every few days? Unh-uh, I couldn't stand that . . . "

"My husband? Who are you talking about?"

"Freddie, who else? The guy loves you. He's so jealous he had me shadowed. And if it hadn't been for that, I wouldn't have solved this mess."

"Yes," said Linda, thoughtfully. "That was rather intriguing about Freddie. I didn't know he had it in him." She came across the room, kissed Johnny on the mouth and said:

"So long, Johnny. And good luck!"

THE END

Other titles in the
Ulverscroft Large Print Series:

TO FIGHT THE WILD
Rod Ansell and Rachel Percy

Lost in uncharted Australian bush, Rod Ansell survived by hunting and trapping wild animals, improvising shelter and using all the bushman's skills he knew.

COROMANDEL
Pat Barr

India in the 1830s is a hot, uncomfortable place, where the East India Company still rules. Amelia and her new husband find themselves caught up in the animosities which seethe between the old order and the new.

THE SMALL PARTY
Lillian Beckwith

A frightening journey to safety begins for Ruth and her small party as their island is caught up in the dangers of armed insurrection.

THE WILDERNESS WALK
Sheila Bishop

Stifling unpleasant memories of a misbegotten romance in Cleave with Lord Francis Aubrey, Lavinia goes on holiday there with her sister. The two women are thrust into a romantic intrigue involving none other than Lord Francis.

THE RELUCTANT GUEST
Rosalind Brett

Ann Calvert went to spend a month on a South African farm with Theo Borland and his sister. They both proved to be different from her first idea of them, and there was Storr Peterson — the most disturbing man she had ever met.

ONE ENCHANTED SUMMER
Anne Tedlock Brooks

A tale of mystery and romance and a girl who found both during one enchanted summer.

CLOUD OVER MALVERTON
Nancy Buckingham

Dulcie soon realises that something is seriously wrong at Malverton, and when violence strikes she is horrified to find herself under suspicion of murder.

AFTER THOUGHTS
Max Bygraves

The Cockney entertainer tells stories of his East End childhood, of his RAF days, and his post-war showbusiness successes and friendships with fellow comedians.

MOONLIGHT
AND MARCH ROSES
D. Y. Cameron

Lynn's search to trace a missing girl takes her to Spain, where she meets Clive Hendon. While untangling the situation, she untangles her emotions and decides on her own future.

NURSE ALICE IN LOVE
Theresa Charles

Accepting the post of nurse to little Fernie Sherrod, Alice Everton could not guess at the romance, suspense and danger which lay ahead at the Sherrod's isolated estate.

POIROT INVESTIGATES
Agatha Christie

Two things bind these eleven stories together — the brilliance and uncanny skill of the diminutive Belgian detective, and the stupidity of his Watson-like partner, Captain Hastings.

LET LOOSE THE TIGERS
Josephine Cox

Queenie promised to find the long-lost son of the frail, elderly murderess, Hannah Jason. But her enquiries threatened to unlock the cage where crucial secrets had long been held captive.